PUFFIN BOOKS

Andrew Norriss was born in Scotland in 1947, went to university in Ireland and taught history in a sixth-form college in England for ten years before becoming a full-time writer. In the course of twenty years, he has written and co-written some hundred and fifty episodes of situation comedies and children's drama for television, and has written six books for children, including *Aquila*, which won the Whitbread Children's Book of the Year in 1997.

He lives very contentedly with his wife and two children in a village in Hampshire, where he acts in the local dramatic society (average age sixty-two), sings in the church choir (average age seventy-two) and for real excitement travels to the cinema in Basingstoke.

Books by Andrew Norriss

AQUILA
BERNARD'S WATCH
THE PORTAL
THE TOUCHSTONE
THE UNLUCKIEST BOY IN THE WORLD

ANDREW NORRISS

THE PORTAL

Best wishes, Bethany!

from

Andrew Norriss

PUFFIN

*For my niece, Lucy, and her mum – either of whom
could probably manage several star portals with
both hands tied behind their backs . . .*

PUFFIN BOOKS

Published by the Penguin Group
Penguin Books Ltd, 80 Strand, London WC2R ORL, England
Penguin Group (USA) Inc., 375 Hudson Street, New York, New York 10014, USA
Penguin Group (Canada), 90 Eglinton Avenue East, Suite 700, Toronto, Ontario, Canada M4P 2Y3
(a division of Pearson Penguin Canada Inc.)
Penguin Ireland, 25 St Stephen's Green, Dublin 2, Ireland (a division of Penguin Books Ltd)
Penguin Group (Australia), 250 Camberwell Road, Camberwell, Victoria 3124, Australia
(a division of Pearson Australia Group Pty Ltd)
Penguin Books India Pvt Ltd, 11 Community Centre, Panchsheel Park, New Delhi – 110 017, India
Penguin Group (NZ), 67 Apollo Drive, Rosedale, North Shore 0632, New Zealand
(a division of Pearson New Zealand Ltd)
Penguin Books (South Africa) (Pty) Ltd, 24 Sturdee Avenue, Rosebank, Johannesburg 2196,
South Africa

Penguin Books Ltd, Registered Offices: 80 Strand, London WC2R ORL, England

puffinbooks.com

First published 2007
1

Text copyright © Andrew Norriss, 2007
All rights reserved

The moral right of the author has been asserted

Typeset in Plantin by Palimpsest Book Production Limited,
Grangemouth, Stirlingshire
Made and printed in England by Clays Ltd, St Ives plc

British Library Cataloguing in Publication Data
A CIP catalogue record for this book is available from the British Library

ISBN: 978-0-141-32158-5

CHAPTER ONE

You tend to remember the day your parents disappear. It's one of those things that stick in the mind. Even years later, William found he could recall not only the day and the date, but things like what shoes his mother had been wearing, and the headline in the newspaper his father had been reading at breakfast.

Most of that day had been perfectly normal. After breakfast, William and Daniel had gone to school as usual. At four o'clock, the bus had delivered them back to the bottom of the road, as usual. They had watched Mrs Duggan's dog, Timber, collect Amy, as usual, then walked up the lane to the house, pushed their way in through the back door . . . and after that, nothing was ever normal again.

On a normal day, there would have been bread and butter set out on the kitchen table, and Mrs Seward would have been standing by the stove, putting two eggs into a saucepan to boil as she smiled a greeting and told Daniel not to leave his bag on the floor. Then Dad would have appeared from his office and asked how things were in the big wide world of school, while he filled the kettle and made the tea.

That was how it was supposed to be. That was how it had always been.

Until now.

'Where are they?' asked Daniel.

'Maybe they're working,' said William, and he buzzed the intercom on the wall, which connected to Dad's office at the other end of the house. But there was no reply. Which could either mean he was busy, or that he wasn't there.

Daniel went out to the hall and pushed open the door to the dining room. Their mother's plant books were spread out on the table – she was halfway through an Open University degree in botany – but there was no sign of Mrs Seward. The two of them went all through the house, calling for her, and then did the same outside, checking the barn and the outhouses before coming back to the kitchen.

'Looks like they had to go out,' said William,

though without much conviction, because they both knew Mr and Mrs Seward never went out. Not together. They went out one at a time to the shops, or to take the boys to the cinema, but there was always one of them left in the house. There had to be, because of Dad's work. It was why they never all went on holiday together. There *always* had to be someone in the house.

William looked round the kitchen to see if there was a note or anything that might explain what had happened, but there was nothing.

'Are you going to ring the number?' asked Daniel.

'Not yet,' said William. 'We don't know if it's a real emergency.'

But two hours later, when there was still no sign of his parents, he gave in and picked up the phone.

William wasn't sure when Dad first told him about the number, but it must have been when he was very young. He could remember his father's big square hands showing him how to push the buttons on the special work-phone in the hall, and explaining how the numbers he should press were written on a piece of card pinned to the wall above it.

'If anything goes wrong,' his father had told

him, 'if there's any sort of emergency, that's what you do, OK?'

When he was older, William had asked what sort of emergency his father had in mind, but Mr Seward only laughed. 'There won't be any emergency,' he had said, 'but if there is, that's the number of the people I work for. They'll know what to do.'

At half past six, William rang the number and was a little disappointed when all he got was an answering machine.

'Hi,' said a woman's voice. 'You have reached the office of Lawrence Kingston. Please leave a message, and he'll get back to you as soon as he can.'

William left a message. He said who he was, where he lived, and that he was a little concerned by the fact that his parents seemed to have disappeared. They might simply have gone out for a walk, but if they had it was unusual and . . . he was concerned.

Two hours later, there was no reply from Mr Kingston, still no sign of his parents, and William did the only other thing he could think of and rang Mrs Duggan.

'I was wondering if you knew what was going on,' he said, after he'd explained the situation. 'Like where they might have gone.'

'No,' said Mrs Duggan, who was a woman of few words.

'They didn't say anything to you about going out? Or something they had to do?'

'No,' Mrs Duggan repeated. Then, after a pause, she added, 'You want me to come up?'

'Yes,' said William. 'Yes, I would.'

Mrs Duggan was a large, red-faced woman, with frizzy hair tied into a bunch at the back of her head, and dressed in bib-fronted dungarees tucked into a pair of wellingtons.

'Still not here?' she asked.

'No,' said William.

Mrs Duggan looked carefully round the kitchen. 'They didn't leave a note or anything?'

'I've looked,' said William, 'but I can't find one.'

'Your dad's office?'

'It's locked.'

Mrs Duggan nodded. The office was usually locked, whether Mr Seward was working in it or not. 'Rung the number yet?' she asked. 'The emergency one?'

William was surprised that Mrs Duggan knew about the number, but said yes, he had dialled it, and left a message.

'Do you think I should ring the police or something?' he asked.

'No,' said Mrs Duggan. 'Don't think your dad would like that.' She thought for a moment. 'Might be a good idea if I stayed here tonight. That OK with you?'

'Yes,' said William. 'Thank you.' It was odd how much better he felt at the thought of having someone else in the house.

'I'll get Amy.' Mrs Duggan headed for the door again. 'And I'll take a look around outside. Check everything's OK.'

Mrs Duggan's daughter, Amy, arrived at the back door ten minutes later carrying a small overnight bag. She was dressed entirely in pink – pink shoes, pink jeans that hung low on her hips, a crop top decorated with glittering, pink beads, and a pink band in her hair framing a face that some would have thought had rather too much make-up for an eight-year-old.

Timber, Mrs Duggan's black-and-white collie, was with her. The dog waited until William had taken Amy inside, before going off to find his mistress.

'Mum says we're staying here tonight,' said Amy, 'because your parents have disappeared.'

'Yes,' said William.

'What's happened to them?'

'I don't know,' said William. 'Daniel's in his room, OK?'

6

Daniel had bunk beds in his bedroom and Amy had often slept there before. The two children were almost the same age and spent a good deal of time together, though William sometimes wondered what a girl like Amy could possibly have in common with a boy whose main interest in life was collecting the skulls of dead animals.

While Amy went upstairs, he waited in the kitchen for Mrs Duggan, who appeared a little later with Timber.

'Done the henhouse,' she said.

'Oh, thank you.' William had forgotten the chickens. His mother was the one who usually made sure they were locked up for the night.

'Had a good look round while I was at it,' Mrs Duggan continued. 'All looks like it should.' She glanced at the clock. 'Nearly nine. Think I'll make up a bed on the sofa and turn in.'

William watched television in his bedroom for an hour before going to bed himself. He lay there, staring at the ceiling, his mind running through some of the things that could have happened to his parents, none of them very pleasant. It wasn't easy to sleep, but he must have dozed off at some point because he was suddenly aware that he could hear voices. The clock by his bed said it was seven minutes past midnight and, throwing on a dressing gown, he came downstairs to find Mrs Duggan talking to a man in the hallway.

The man was elderly, with a head of closely cropped white hair and a trim white beard that framed a pair of startlingly blue eyes. He was dressed in a loosely hanging, rather crumpled suit, and mopped at his face with a large spotted hand-kerchief. His face lit up in a smile when he saw William.

'Well, well, well!' He held out a hand in greeting. 'Look at you! Almost a young man!'

'Who are you?' said William.

'This is your Uncle Larry,' said Mrs Duggan.

'My uncle?' William looked at her blankly. 'Are you sure?'

'I'm not, strictly speaking, a blood relative,' said Uncle Larry, 'but that's what your father used to call me, when he was little.' He shook William's hand. 'Lawrence Kingston. Your parents and I go back a long way.'

'Do you know what's happened to them?' asked William.

'I do indeed.' Uncle Larry reached into his jacket pocket. 'And I have a letter for you from them.'

'They've gone on holiday,' said Mrs Duggan.

William stared at her.

'It's all in here.' Uncle Larry held out an

envelope. 'When you read it, you'll realize there's nothing to worry about.'

The envelope had *To William & Daniel* written on the front in his mother's handwriting and inside William found a single sheet of paper, also in his mother's writing. It said:

My dearest boys,

By the time you get this, your father and I will be somewhere in France! Dad suddenly decided this morning that what we really needed was a break and next thing you know he's packing a suitcase and we're heading for a campsite in the Alps!

We're not sure how long we'll be gone. Probably only a few days (but you never know!) and Uncle Larry has very kindly offered to look after you both while we're gone. BE GOOD! And remember he'll be looking after Dad's business as well, so try and help him in any way you can and make sure you do whatever he tells you.

We shall miss you both, but we'll send a card and maybe try and phone once we get there, but we shall have lots to tell you about when we get back. What an adventure, eh?

With love,
Mum.

William read the letter twice without speaking.

'They haven't said how long they're going to be away,' he said.

'No,' Uncle Larry agreed. 'I suppose that depends on how it goes. They might be back in a day or two, maybe a week. Let's hope they enjoy themselves, eh?'

'How did they get there?'

'I'm sorry?' Uncle Larry blinked.

'To France,' said William. 'How did they get there?'

'They flew.' Uncle Larry took a deep breath. 'Look, I'm sorry. This is all my fault. If I'd been here when I promised, you wouldn't have had all these hours of worry. Unfortunately, after your parents had gone, I realized there were all these things I'd need from the flat. So I went home to get them, thought I'd just lie down for a few minutes to catch my breath and next thing I knew I'd . . . I'd fallen asleep.' He gave an embarrassed laugh. 'I still can't believe I slept for that long, but I did. It's been a heavy week, you see, and . . . and I was tired.'

He looked tired, thought William.

'I do apologize. The last thing I wanted to do was upset either yourself or Daniel.'

Before William could reply, the telephone rang. It was Dad's work-phone, not the ordinary one, and Uncle Larry answered it. He listened for a moment then replaced the receiver.

'It's back to work for me, I'm afraid!' He turned to Mrs Duggan. 'Perhaps you could make William a hot drink or something to help him sleep. I'll be about an hour. If either of you wants to stay up and talk, that's fine, but it might be better to save it till tomorrow.'

He walked off down the hall into Dad's office, and William noticed that he didn't seem to need a key.

Mrs Duggan led the way into the kitchen, Timber padding silently beside her. She collected a pint of milk from the fridge and a saucepan from the cupboard by the stove.

'You've not met your uncle before?'

'Not that I remember,' said William. 'Have you?'

'Oh, yes.' Mrs Duggan found two mugs and a jar of cocoa. 'And for what it's worth I reckon you can trust him. Your dad did.'

William didn't answer. Uncle Larry might be the sort of person you could trust and he might not, but he knew one thing with a cold certainty that sat in his stomach like an undigested meal.

Whatever else he was doing, Uncle Larry was lying through his teeth.

CHAPTER TWO

At breakfast the next morning, Daniel had no trouble accepting the fact that his parents had decided on the spur of the moment to take a holiday in France. He read the letter from his mother, put it to one side, poured himself a bowl of cereal and asked if he would be allowed to go skull-hunting after school. He seemed all set to carry on as if everything was still normal.

But it wasn't.

For a start, when they got back from school, there was still no tea on the table. Although Uncle Larry had found some butter, he had failed to find any bread or even to get water out of the tap to fill a saucepan and boil the eggs. Daniel solved the water problem by explaining how the taps worked – Uncle Larry had been pushing them like a button, instead of turning the handle – but neither of them could find any bread. They must have finished the last of it at breakfast and William remembered that Friday was the day his mother usually went shopping.

'Shopping?' Uncle Larry tugged thoughtfully at his beard. 'What would that involve exactly?'

'You go to Tesco,' said Daniel, 'and buy all the food we'll need for the next week.'

'I might need a bit of help with that one,' said Uncle Larry. 'Do either of you know where this "Tesco" is?'

They took Dad's car to the supermarket, and the drive was a nightmare. Uncle Larry gave a fair impression of someone who had never been in a car before in his life. You could almost see him working out where to put the key, and which pedal made it go forwards. For the first two miles, they went so slowly that they were overtaken not only by a tractor, but by a child on a bicycle and two women out jogging. It was embarrassing but, as Uncle Larry's confidence increased and he began to speed up, it got worse.

'Getting the hang of it now,' he murmured, and a few minutes later was driving at seventy miles an hour, mostly on the wrong side of the road, still in third gear. Daniel sat in the back, shrieking with laughter, while William closed his eyes and prayed they would get there without killing too many pedestrians.

At Tesco's car park, Uncle Larry parked neatly in a bay for the disabled and peered over the steering wheel at the swarms of people moving in and out of the main entrance. 'I think you might manage this sort of thing best on your own,' he said, reaching into his jacket for a wallet. 'How much money will you need?'

William had no idea, so Uncle Larry gave him three hundred pounds from an astonishingly thick wad of notes, and told him to come back if he needed any more.

Daniel had never been happier. On the odd occasions he had been shopping with his mother, Mrs Seward had refused to buy anything that wasn't already on her list. Now, however, he could put whatever caught his fancy into the trolley. In no time, it was packed with frozen pizzas, pots of chocolate trifles, cans of cola and dozens of bags of crisps. William was the one who tried to remember they might need things like bread and pots of marmalade as well.

Uncle Larry, when they got back to the car, made no protest about any of the purchases, or the price. His only concern, as they loaded the bags into the back of the Toyota, was whether they had enough to keep them from starving over the next few days.

Fortunately, while they were shopping, he had found a copy of the Highway Code in the glove compartment and reminded himself of some of the rules of the road, so the journey home was a little more sedate but, once they got there, the boys were left to themselves again.

'Sorry about this,' he said as he marched off down the hall to answer Dad's work-phone. 'Looks like more work. You can sort out a meal for yourselves, can you?'

'This is great, isn't it!' said Daniel delightedly. 'We can eat whatever we want. He doesn't care!'

It was true that Uncle Larry didn't worry about what the boys ate or, it later transpired, what they watched on television or when they went to bed. But it wasn't that he didn't care. He came out of Dad's office several times in the course of the evening to check that they were all right and to ask if there was anything they needed. It was obvious that, if there had been a problem, Uncle Larry would have done his best to solve it, but he never *told* them what they should be doing. It was, William thought, as if he didn't know.

For Daniel, it was heaven, but William was less sure. He had a feeling they should not have been left to buy their own food, to leave it unpacked in bags around the kitchen or to choose what they would eat for supper. Someone should have been there to tell them that a box of chocolates was not a proper meal, that Friday evening was when you were supposed to make a start on your homework, and that ten o'clock was not the time to start watching *Resident Evil* on the television.

Well, they should be telling Daniel, anyway . . .

The following morning, there was a postcard lying on the mat by the front door. It was a picture of a mountain, its peak shrouded in clouds, and was addressed to *William & Daniel Seward* under a French stamp with a smudged postmark.

William read the message, written in his father's careful handwriting.

Hi! Just arrived and settling in. Our tent is about a mile from this peak and we'll be walking up it this morning. Everything's wonderfully peaceful and calm – just what we needed! Don't forget to help Uncle Larry as much as possible. See you soon! Love, Dad.

It was the card that decided it for William, though he waited till Daniel had gone to see Amy before buzzing the intercom in the kitchen that connected to his father's office.

'Yes?' Uncle Larry's voice, when he eventually answered, sounded as if he had just woken up.

'I need to talk to you,' said William.

'Now?'

'Yes. Now.'

'OK. I'll be right up.' There was a noise like someone yawning, then Uncle Larry broke the connection.

William waited and, a minute or two later, heard the sound of footsteps coming from his father's office, then Uncle Larry appeared in the kitchen. His suit looked more crumpled than ever, and there was a button missing from the jacket.

'Is that from your father?' he asked, pointing to the postcard on the table. 'Are they having a good time?'

'I'd like to know what's really happened to them,' said William.

'I'm sorry?' Uncle Larry looked startled.

'My parents,' said William. 'I want to know what's happened to them.'

'Well,' said Uncle Larry, 'if you read the post-card, I'm sure –'

'The postcard's a fake,' William interrupted. 'It takes more than a day to get a postcard from France and, even if they broke all the records, it still wouldn't have arrived yet because the post doesn't come till midday on a Saturday.'

'Ah . . .' Uncle Larry made a vague gesture with his hands. 'Maybe today, the postman –'

'Look, I know my parents haven't gone on holiday,' William interrupted firmly. 'Apart from the postcard, all their clothes are still hanging in the cupboards. Dad's walking shoes are in the porch. Mum's got an essay due in on Monday which is still sitting on the dining-room table, half-finished. Their passports are both still in the drawer and, if they ever *did* decide to go on holiday, I can't believe they'd leave us with someone who can't drive, can't shop and doesn't even know how to turn on a tap. I'm not saying you're a bad person, and Mrs Duggan says that Dad trusted you, but whatever's going on, it's not what you said and I want to know the truth.'

There was a long silence.

'Well?' said William eventually. 'Where are they?'

Uncle Larry gave a long sigh, pulled out a chair and sat down. When he finally spoke it was in a low, rather depressed voice. 'I don't know,' he said. 'I've spent most of the last thirty-six hours trying to find out, and I still have no idea where your parents are. I wish I did, but I don't.'

Mrs Duggan stood halfway up the hill, staring thoughtfully down at the view. The big farmhouse where the Sewards lived was over to her left, her own cottage was directly below, and all the rest was fields and woodland, with the lane winding through it down to the main road.

At the junction, she could see the tiny figures of Daniel and Amy crouching over something on the tarmac. Probably a dead animal of some sort, she thought. There wasn't a lot of traffic on these roads, but enough to mow down the occasional rabbit or pigeon. It should keep them happy for an hour or two.

Both the view and the children, however, occupied only a tiny part of her thoughts. The deeper worry, the one that nagged like a toothache at the back of her mind, was whether or not she should tell William what she knew about his parents.

Part of her said that she should – she suspected he didn't believe the story about them going on holiday anyway – but another part pointed out that she had promised not to say anything. And a promise to Jack Seward was not something she took lightly. Not after all he'd done for her.

And how would telling William help anyway? It might just leave him more confused than he was already. Once again, she was forced to the conclusion that the best thing was to say nothing – at least for the moment – and see how things turned out. If it looked like they were going badly off the rails, then she might step in, but in the meantime she would wait. Keep an eye on things, obviously, but wait.

Down in the valley, she could see Timber emerging from the workshop and beginning the long climb up the hill towards her. She'd sent him down to get a hammer, so they could do some fencing up by the quarry. She hoped he had the right tool this time. Yesterday, when she sent him off for a bucket of nails, he'd come back with a set of socket spanners . . .

'You have no idea where they've gone?' William followed Uncle Larry down the hall towards his father's office. 'No idea at all?'

'Well, I have an *idea*,' said Uncle Larry, 'but even if it's right, I don't know why they've gone there without telling anyone.' He pushed open the door and waited until William had followed him inside. 'Have you been in here before?'

William nodded. He had been in his father's office on several occasions, though it was not something his parents encouraged. If Dad was making a business call, people bursting in and asking questions didn't give the best impression of professionalism and efficiency. That was why they had the intercom from the kitchen.

'Did your father ever tell you what he does for a living?'

'He's a shipping broker.' William was a little vague on the details but he knew roughly what this meant. 'If people want something shipped or flown anywhere, he's the one who arranges it for them.'

'Yes . . .' Uncle Larry nodded. 'That's the cover story.' He stepped across the office to the desk under the window, picked up the phone, and began tapping in a number. 'And I'm afraid the truth is going to come as a bit of a shock. Normally, I'd take a bit of time to prepare you for this, but in the circumstances I think we just have to dive straight in . . .'

As he pressed the final button, a section of wall on the right of the room disappeared. One moment there was a wall with a picture and a skirting board, and the next there was an opening to a space the size of a broom cupboard.

'If you'd like to join me?' Uncle Larry had replaced the phone on the desk and was already stepping into the space. 'All perfectly safe, I promise.'

William opened his mouth to speak, then changed his mind and, after a moment's hesitation, walked over to join him. As he stepped inside, the floor disappeared and he found himself dropping through empty space.

'It's a lift,' said Uncle Larry, shouting so that

he could be heard over the noise of William's scream. 'Takes us down a couple of hundred feet. Quite fun when you get used to it. There we are, you see?'

The floor had reappeared and a dazed William looked out into a large circular room with a stairwell in the centre and a series of doors running round the outside.

'This is William,' said Uncle Larry, stepping out into the room. 'I'm just going to show him around, OK?'

'Yes, of course, Larry.' The voice was a woman's, soft and gentle. 'Welcome to the station, William.'

William looked round, but couldn't see who was speaking. It was hard to tell, but the voice seemed to be coming from the ceiling.

'If you could say something,' said Uncle Larry, 'so Emma can recognize your voice? She's in charge of security, you see.'

'Why . . . Where . . . What is this place?' said William.

'Thank you. Now . . .' Uncle Larry pointed to the first door on their left. 'That's what your dad calls his pantry.' He pointed to the other doors in turn. 'Kitchen, wardrobe, recreation room, main reception and visitors' suites, but the important bit . . . is over here.'

He walked briskly to a doorway on the far side, pushed it open, and waited for William to follow him inside.

The room was about ten metres long, wider at the far end than it was near the door, and entirely white. The walls, the floor and the ceiling all seemed to be of the same material, with no visible join where they met. It was brightly lit, though William could not see where the light was coming from, and the only furniture was a single, heavily upholstered chair by the wall on the right. Above it was a hook, on which hung a large white dressing gown of the sort provided by upmarket hotels.

In the centre of the room was what looked like a pool, set into the middle of the floor. It was circular, about two metres in diameter and the lip, made of the same material as the walls and floor, was about fifteen centimetres high. Inside, there was a milky liquid that rippled and swirled, though the more he looked at it, the more William wondered if it was really a liquid at all, and then he found that staring at it made him slightly seasick.

'That's where your parents went.' Uncle Larry pointed at the pool. 'At least I think it is.'

'What . . . what is it?' asked William.

'It's a Portal,' said Uncle Larry. 'A Star Portal.'

CHAPTER THREE

'The Portals,' Uncle Larry explained, 'are the glue that binds together the worlds of the Federation.'

He was sitting on a swivel chair in the room he had described as Mr Seward's 'pantry', pointing to a chart on the wall that was densely covered in lines and dots.

'It's a bit like a spider's web, you see? The dots where these lines join are the Portals and if you jump into a Portal here,' he tapped his finger on one of the dots, 'the marvels of time-tunnel technology mean you will instantly come out here.' He tapped at the next dot in the web. 'You follow?'

William nodded. There was no problem understanding what Uncle Larry was telling him. It was *believing* it that was the tricky bit.

'The only limitation is that if you build a tunnel longer than three or four light years, what comes out this end may not be *exactly* what went in at the other, which can be a little discouraging for passengers. So out here on the Rim, where your Federation worlds might be anything up to twenty light years apart, every four parsecs, you have a booster station like this one, and your star traveller comes back into real space for six hours, lets his ankles get back to their proper size, rehydrates, and then . . . carries on.'

Alongside the chart on the wall, William noticed, was a cork board covered in photographs. There were dozens of them. Mostly pictures of his father with men and women that William had never met. No, that wasn't entirely true. Looking closer he found he did recognize some of the faces. They belonged to people who had visited his father on business, or shared his mother's interest in plants. She was in some of the pictures as well, standing in the garden or in the kitchen upstairs, laughing. You could actually *see* her laughing, because if you looked at any of the pictures long enough, the images began to move . . .

'Near the Hub, of course,' Uncle Larry indicated a spot at the centre of the chart, 'you've got these vast star gates throwing out capsules of half a million passengers at a time, but out here on the Rim the Portals are mostly used for transporting bricks, and we don't get more than two or three passengers a week. But you still need someone to manage the place . . . and that's where your dad came in.'

A lot of the pictures, William noticed, had been signed. 'Thanks for everything, Jack!' 'To Jack and Lois, with all best wishes, Ambassador B'Wwath.' 'Good luck, Jack! And thanks for all the fish!'

'I mean, you *could* build a station in deep space, bring in all the raw materials and supplies, then try and find someone who doesn't mind living there on his own for thirty years . . .' Uncle Larry gave a dismissive snort. 'But it's a lot simpler if you can find a planet that already has most of the things you need and someone who already lives there.'

At the bottom, William noticed, there was a picture of himself on his last birthday, sitting at the kitchen table with his mother. And another of Daniel, with the sheep's skull that had started his latest obsession, and others, more faded and creased, that dated right back to when they were both toddlers and learning to walk.

'And the customers love it, of course! It gives them a glimpse of a native culture that under normal circumstances they'd never be allowed to visit. So everyone's happy and the only thing a supervisor like me has to do is call in occasionally to sort out any problems.' Uncle Larry paused and looked thoughtfully at his feet. 'Like this one.'

To Daniel's delight, the dead bird was a magpie. He didn't have a magpie skull and the head was quite undamaged. He'd cut it from the body with his penknife, and was now burying it in an ants' nest. When he came back in a week or so, the bones and beak would have been picked clean and he could take it home.

Amy watched from a safe distance. She was wearing new jeans with her favourite top, and was anxious not to get blood on either of them.

Daniel carefully marked the spot where he had buried the head, wiped his hands on his trousers and they began walking back up the lane.

'Do you know when your parents are coming back?' asked Amy.

'No,' said Daniel, but privately he hoped it would not be too soon. He was having far too much fun. It was a Saturday morning, and no one had said a word yet about schoolwork, or tidying his room, or cleaning out the henhouse. Life was a lot simpler with no parents.

'You're bleeding,' said Amy.

Daniel looked down and saw there was blood dripping from a finger of his left hand. He must have cut himself when he was cutting up the magpie, he thought, and wondered what he should do.

Amy took a tissue from the sleeve of her T-shirt – it was the purple one with *Bad Attitude* written in black across the front – and wrapped it round Daniel's finger. Then she took the scrunchie from her hair and used it to hold the tissue in place.

'You'll need to wash it when we get home,' she said, 'or it'll get infected.'

If he did fall ill, she thought, she would have to nurse him, and she wondered what she would wear. Uniforms could be quite attractive if they fitted properly. Maybe her mother could make one of those blue tunics, and the white hat thing would be interesting . . .

'When I came over after getting your message,' said Uncle Larry, 'I realized there were only three places your parents could have gone.'

He was standing in the kitchen area of the station, next door to the pantry. It was large and well-equipped, though a little cluttered at the moment as no one had done the washing-up for a couple of days.

'My first thought was that they'd gone outside somewhere. They're not supposed to both leave the farm at the same time but we all bend the rules occasionally, and I thought maybe they fancied a trip out or something.' Uncle Larry chose a mug that seemed slightly less dirty than the others and held it under the spout of a machine that, with a great deal of hissing, produced a trickle of hot water on to a tea bag. 'Except they hadn't.'

'How do you know?' asked William.

'There's a perimeter fence round the farm,' said Uncle Larry. 'Part of the security system. It tracks anyone coming in and out. Emma says neither of them left the farm bounds, and I've searched the house and the grounds and there's not a trace of them.' He sipped his tea and grimaced. 'So . . . the second possibility was that they were somewhere in the station – maybe they'd had an accident and were lying somewhere, injured. But I've searched both floors, all the engine rooms, storerooms, access shafts – and they're not here either. Which only leaves option three.'

'They've gone through the Portal?'

'Exactly.' Uncle Larry frowned. 'Though I still can't believe it. I mean, why? And your dad of all people . . .'

'If they did go through the Portal,' said William, 'where would they have gone?'

'There's only two places they could go.' Uncle Larry carried his tea out to the central hall and back to the pantry, where he stood in front of the star chart on the wall. 'Upline to Q'Vaar, or downline to Byroid V. Now, they can't have gone up. The station manager on Q'Vaar was standing next to the Portal that entire afternoon as part of a practice medical emergency and he'd have seen them. However, it's *just* possible they went to Byroid V.' He pointed to the map. 'It's where three lines join, you see, and if your mum and dad snuck in at the right time, they might have been able to pose as ordinary passengers, and either carry on downline or get lost somewhere on Byroid V itself.'

'Why would they have gone there?' asked William.

Uncle Larry spread out his hands in a gesture of ignorance. 'The only way to answer that is to find them and ask. Which is where you come in.' Uncle Larry looked directly at William.

'Me? What can I do?'

'I need to go to Byroid V and make some enquiries,' said Uncle Larry, 'and I need someone here to do the bricks while I'm gone. It won't be for more than a day. Do you think you could cope?'

'The bricks?'

'Nothing too demanding, I promise.' Uncle Larry took William by the arm and was leading him across the central hallway to the Portal, when he was stopped by a faint buzzing noise. He reached into his pocket and took out a mobile.

'Yes?'

'Uncle Larry?' The voice on the phone was Daniel's. 'I'm hungry. What are we having for lunch?'

Uncle Larry said he had to write a report, so William was the one who went up to sort out lunch.

In the kitchen, he made some cheese on toast for Daniel and Amy, persuaded Daniel to put a dressing and some cream on the cut on his finger and tried to stop his brain from endlessly going over the impossible things it had absorbed that morning.

While they were eating, Mrs Duggan appeared.

'How's it going?' she asked.

'Fine,' said William. 'Thank you.'

Mrs Duggan nodded. 'Your uncle around?'

'He's . . . working,' said William. 'Did you want him for something?'

'Wasn't urgent,' said Mrs Duggan.

There was a muffled bark from outside and she opened the door. Timber trotted in with a basket of eggs in his teeth.

'Got him to check the henhouse for you,' said Mrs Duggan, putting the basket on the table. She sniffed. 'Need to be down in Bottom Field this afternoon. Wondered if Amy could stay here?'

'Yes, of course,' said William. Amy usually spent most of her time up at the farm anyway.

Mrs Duggan looked round at the bags of shopping that littered the floor. 'Make sure she helps you put this lot away.'

'Right,' said William. 'I'll do that.'

'The bricks,' Uncle Larry explained, 'are how the Federation worlds communicate with each other.'

Using a pair of oven gloves, he held up a black brick, slightly larger and smoother than the household variety, that had emerged from the Portal a few seconds before, like Arthur's sword rising from the lake.

'In fact, they're what makes the Federation possible.' Uncle Larry tossed the brick in the air and caught it as he walked over to the wall. 'In here, we have dispatches, trade treaties, legislation, scientific journals, films, newspapers, books, music, poetry, letters, television programmes – there'll be at least a billion separate items on this one brick . . . and your job is to put it in here. You see?'

As he spoke, he dropped the brick into a chute set into the wall at the far end of the room.

'You put it in there so Emma can look at it,

download any information that's specifically for this station, and upload any messages you might want to pass on to anyone else. And you do that every time the bricks come in, which is every ten hours and seventeen minutes.'

There was a gentle grating sound as the brick reappeared on a ledge to the right of the chute. Uncle Larry picked it up and carried it back to the Portal.

'You know how long it takes for a message to travel forty thousand light years from the core of the galaxy to out here on the Rim? *Less than three days!* Can you believe that?'

William did his best to look impressed, and waited as Uncle Larry placed the brick in the centre of the Portal, then stood back as it silently sank from view.

'Right.' Uncle Larry took off the oven gloves and passed them to William. 'That was the brick going upline, and in a minute or two we'll get the one going down. Think you can manage?'

William took the gloves and, a minute and a half later, watched as the downline brick rose up through the milky surface of the Portal with a faint *blup* noise and sat there. He stepped forward and took it. It was lighter than he expected and he could feel the warmth even through the gloves as he carried it over to the chute and dropped it in. A moment later, it reappeared on a ledge to one side and he carried it back to the Portal.

'On a station like this, most days, there won't be anything specifically for us,' said Uncle Larry, 'but we give it to Emma all the same. One of the things she does is take a copy in case something goes wrong. Not that it ever does. But we don't take chances with the bricks. Too important.' He nodded happily as the brick disappeared below the surface of the Portal with the same ease with which it had arrived. 'Now . . . You know when the next one gets here?'

Uncle Larry had said that the time between bricks was ten hours and seventeen minutes, and William did a brief calculation in his head.

'Twenty-four minutes past midnight,' he said.

'Well done.' Uncle Larry took off his jacket, dropped it on the floor and began unbuttoning his shirt. 'You don't have to remember the exact time because Emma'll give you a ring ten minutes beforehand. I gave you the phone, didn't I?'

William held up the mobile.

'Good. And you remember the number?'

'1066,' said William.

'Right.' Uncle Larry threw his shirt on to his jacket and began taking off his trousers. 'Make sure you don't go too far from the house. You don't want to be late. Any questions?'

'I don't think so,' said William.

'There're no passengers booked in till Tuesday, so it's only the bricks tonight you have to worry about. The next ones aren't till eleven in the morning and I'll be back long before then!' Uncle Larry stood there, his wrinkled body clad only in a pair of shorts. 'Don't forget, any problems, you ask Emma.'

William nodded.

'But there won't be any problems.' Uncle Larry stepped forward to stand in the middle of the Portal. 'You'll be fine. And when you wake up in the morning, I'll be here with news about your parents!'

He gave a brief wave and, like a swimmer diving into a pool, sank straight into the floor and disappeared from sight.

CHAPTER FOUR

Illiam stood there for a moment, staring at the empty surface of the Portal, before bending down to pick up the clothes that were scattered over the floor. Now he knew why Uncle Larry's suit was always so crumpled, he thought, and wondered where would be the best place to put them.

'I would suggest the laundry drawer,' said Emma, from somewhere in the ceiling.

The voice made William jump – he wasn't aware that he'd spoken out loud – but the suggestion seemed reasonable. 'Where's the laundry drawer?' he asked.

'Third door on the right,' said Emma.

William made his way back out to the lobby, turned right, walked along to the third door and found the wedge-shaped room in front of him was filled almost entirely with clothes. There were literally hundreds of items – suits and jackets, trousers and skirts, coats and jeans – all hanging on racks that filled most of the floor space and with more suspended from the ceiling above.

'The laundry drawer is on your left,' said Emma. 'You pull the handle under the red arrow and place any items that require cleaning inside.'

William walked over to the wall, pulled the handle under the red arrow and pushed Uncle Larry's clothes inside. Emma told him that cleaning would be complete in approximately ten minutes and, sure enough, the suit and shirt came out ten minutes later, not only pressed and cleaned but with the missing button replaced on the jacket.

'Does Uncle Larry have a room down here?' he asked.

'He's in the blue suite,' said Emma. 'Fourth door on the left.'

William carried the clothes back out to the lobby and walked round to the fourth door on his left, just past the Portal. It led into a large, comfortable room with a bed on one side, a couple of armchairs and a table on the other, and a door at the far end that led through to the bathroom.

The room was extremely untidy. The bed was unmade, there were towels and clothes scattered over the floor, and the table was littered with plates of half-eaten food and dirty cups. William hung Uncle Larry's clothes in one of the cupboards and went back out to the lobby.

It was time, he thought, to do a little exploring.

There were nine doors opening from the central lobby. Moving clockwise, the two doors after the Portal and Uncle Larry's bedroom led to two more guest rooms, one decorated mostly in green and the other in yellow. After that, there was the lift and Dad's 'pantry', and then the kitchen which, William discovered, had a storeroom at the back containing an impressive range of food and drink.

Along from the kitchen was the room with all the clothes and the laundry drawer. Next to that was a recreation room with a full-sized snooker table, a small gymnasium and some pinball machines, and the last door before William was back at the Portal opened into a room that was at least twice the size of any of the others he had seen.

It was a sitting room, with two enormous sofas facing each other in the centre, a set of dining chairs grouped round a table in one corner, and a circle of armchairs in another. Around the walls there was a drinks cabinet, several bookcases, a television, and a vast collection of DVDs – but the real surprise for William was what he saw through the windows that ran along the back. They looked out on exactly the view you would get from the sitting room of the farmhouse above.

Standing in front of them, he could see the lawn and flower beds directly ahead, the barn over to the left and the field that ran down to the river on the right. The whole picture looked completely real. The trees were swaying in the breeze, the sheep in the fields on the other side of the valley bent their heads as they grazed and, when he asked, Emma explained that he was seeing a real time image of exactly what you would see if you were upstairs in the farmhouse, transferred to the screen below.

Not that it looked like a screen. Even right up close the illusion was complete. There was a slight haze on the field over to the right, you could see every detail in the swirls of the dust the chickens were kicking up in their pen and you could even see the little drips of oil coming from the chainsaw Daniel was carrying across to the barn . . .

William paused.

A chainsaw.

Daniel had a chainsaw . . .

William's brother did not like being told that he couldn't use the saw.

'I need it,' he protested, 'to cut up this wood.'

39

'It's a chainsaw,' said William, 'and you're eight. You know perfectly well you can't use it. I'm five years older than you and *I'm* not allowed to touch it.'

'Uncle Larry said I could.'

'Uncle Larry would let you set fire to your bedroom if he thought it would keep you quiet,' said William. 'What were you trying to do with it anyway?'

'I'm making shelves.' Daniel kicked at the dirt with his feet. 'And I can't cut up the planks without a saw, can I?'

Amy appeared at the barn door with Timber, carrying an overnight bag.

'Is it all right then?' she asked.

William turned to her. 'Is what all right?'

'Daniel was supposed to be asking if I could sleep over again tonight,' said Amy. 'Mum says she's going to be out lambing.'

'There's no point asking him,' said Daniel crossly. 'He won't let anybody do anything.'

'Yes, of course you can stay,' said William.

'Great!' Amy smiled. 'And she says did she leave her tool-belt here the other night?'

'I think it's in the kitchen,' said William, and he was about to walk back to the house to get it, when Timber trotted past him and pushed open the back door. He came back out a moment later with the tool-belt in his mouth and William thought, not for the first time, that there was something a bit creepy about a dog that understood quite so much of what people said.

It turned out Daniel wanted a set of shelves so that he would have somewhere to display his collection of skulls and William suggested that, instead of making them, he use the bookshelves from the spare bedroom. He and Amy helped Daniel carry them through to his room, and William left him setting out the skulls while Amy printed labels to go on the front of each item.

He would have liked to go back to the station, but decided it would not be wise to leave Daniel alone for too long. Instead, he went down to the kitchen and began putting away the shopping. It seemed to take a very long time and he couldn't help thinking that this was not how he normally spent a Saturday afternoon.

On a normal Saturday, he would probably have gone over to Craig's house, or Craig would have come over to the farm. They would have taken the canoe down to the river, or played a game on the computer, or gone to the cinema . . . He wondered if Uncle Larry had found his parents yet. He hoped he had, and that Saturdays would soon be normal again.

William had liked normal.

At supper, Daniel did not eat a great deal – possibly because of the six chocolate cupcakes he had had for tea – and then announced that he and Amy were going upstairs to watch a film on television. William suggested that he had a bath first.

'I don't want a bath,' said Daniel. 'I don't need a bath.'

William pointed to the chocolate smears around his brother's face, the bloodstains on his arms and the sheep dropping that had somehow got caught in his hair.

'Have a bath,' he said, 'before Amy refuses to share a room with you.'

The door to Dad's office opened when he turned the handle, just as Uncle Larry had said it would, and when William tapped 1066 into the phone on the desk, the wall to the right of the window disappeared, revealing the space that led down to the station. He stood in it, the floor disappeared, and a few seconds later he was stepping into the central lobby of the station and being greeted by Emma, who asked if there was anything he needed.

'Not at the moment, thanks,' William told her. 'I'm just going to look around for a bit.'

For almost an hour he wandered in and out of the nine rooms around the lobby. He stood in the wardrobe room, staring at all the clothes and wondering what they were for. He lay on the bed in the green bedroom and stared thoughtfully at the ceiling. He stared at the map of the Federation Star Portals above Dad's desk and then the photos on the cork board beside it. He stared at the surface of the Portal itself until it made him feel queasy again, and then he stood in the sitting room and stared through the window at the sun going down behind the trees on the far side of the valley.

He did a lot of staring.

At eight o'clock, he went back upstairs to see what Daniel and Amy were doing, and found that his brother was already in bed and asleep. Amy was still watching the film, while repainting her toenails, and William made her promise to go to bed when it finished, but said to call him on the intercom if she needed anything.

Back down in the station, there were still nearly four hours before the bricks were due to arrive and he began exploring the station in a little more detail, going through all the rooms again, peering into cupboards and opening hatches. One of his first finds, at the back of Dad's pantry, was a large cupboard with two rows of guns stacked neatly along the wall, and he asked Emma what they were for.

'The weapons are to defend the station in the event of an attack,' she told him.

'Attack?' said William. 'We get attacked?'

'This station has never been the victim of aggression,' said Emma, 'but it is considered wise to be prepared.'

'Can I touch them?' William asked.

The station computer assured him he could take and use any gun he wanted, but in the end he decided not to. It felt a bit like letting Daniel play with a chainsaw.

In an area off the kitchen, William found the machines that were responsible for keeping the station clean – they weren't as exciting as the guns but still interesting – and in the sitting room there was a collection of books on Federation history, with pictures like the photographs on Dad's wall, that moved when you looked at them. Then, in a booth at the back of the recreation room, he discovered what turned out to be the station's equivalent of a games console.

Sitting in the chair, William found himself in the middle, literally, of a battle of epic proportions in which he was the commander of a battlecruiser whose task was to take and hold the fourteen worlds and thirty-seven moons of a star system near the Hub. He was still fighting, two hours later, when Emma told him he was needed at the Portal.

The brick from Byroid V appeared at exactly twenty-four minutes past midnight and William, standing ready with the oven gloves, watched it rise to the surface, before picking it up and placing it carefully in the chute. When it reappeared on the ledge, he carried it back to the Portal and placed it in the centre. Shortly after it had disappeared, the brick from Q'Vaar arrived and William carried that over to the chute as well.

It was all as simple as Uncle Larry had said it would be and he was just stepping into the lift to go upstairs to bed, when Emma announced that there was a message for him. It was from the station manager on Q'Vaar and came in the form of a hologram of a man with black curly hair whose head and shoulders appeared in mid-air above the staircase in the centre of the lobby.

'Hi, Larry!' said the figure. 'Just to let you know General Ghool's coming through a bit earlier than expected. I've told him about Jack and Lois – I hope that's all right – and he's hoping you'll have better news by the time he gets to you at . . .' the figure paused to consult a notepad, '. . . 01.09. OK?'

'Who's General Ghool?' asked William as the hologram disappeared.

'He's an officer in the Federation Peace Force,' said Emma. 'He has been dealing with a crisis that was resolved rather sooner than expected.'

'He's coming here?'

'Yes.'

William looked at his watch. 'In half an hour? What should I do?'

'I have no instructions for your behaviour in this eventuality,' said Emma.

William took a deep breath and thought for a moment. 'OK,' he said, 'what would my dad do if he knew the General was coming through?'

For the next thirty minutes, William was kept busy collecting the dirty plates and mugs from the sitting room – fortunately, washing them was as simple as doing the laundry – getting the right machines to hoover the floor and clean the tables, setting out clean towels and a dressing gown in the green suite and preparing a tray of sandwiches in the kitchen.

At nine minutes past one he was standing by the Portal as the General rose from its surface. There was quite a lot of him to rise. General Ghool was nearly seven feet tall with the bushiest eyebrows William had ever seen and long grey hair, tied neatly in a pigtail at the back.

'Hope you don't mind my being early, Larry.' The General's voice was booming out almost as soon as his head appeared above the surface of the Portal, 'but the Thaliron thing fizzled out as soon as I arrived. Nobody needed shooting so I

46

thought . . .' He paused, looking suspiciously at William from under his eyebrows. 'You're not Larry.'

'No,' William agreed.

'You must be William.' The General stepped out of the Portal. 'Any news of your parents yet?'

'Not yet,' said William. 'Mr Kingston's gone to Byroid V to find out what happened.'

'And left you to man the fort, eh?' The General gave a grunt. 'How's it going?'

William was about to say that it seemed to be going all right, when the phone rang in his pocket. It was Amy, calling from upstairs.

'I think you need to come and see Daniel,' she said, her voice sounding small and rather frightened. 'He's sick.'

CHAPTER FIVE

Daniel certainly looked sick. His face was flushed, he was sweating heavily and his breath came in rapid, panting gasps. When William asked how he was feeling, Daniel didn't answer. It was as if he couldn't hear.

'How long has he been like this?' William asked.

'I don't know.' Amy's face would have been white even without the face pack she was wearing. 'I woke up because he was shouting.'

'OK . . . ' William knew the first thing was to get help. 'I'll call your mother.'

'I tried that,' said Amy. 'There's no answer. She's out lambing.'

If Mrs Duggan was outside looking after a sheep giving birth, William thought, finding her would not be easy. She had a mobile, but there were places on the farm where reception was poor or non-existent and going outside to look for her would take far too long . . .

'Should we call an ambulance?' asked Amy.

William knew calling the emergency services was the obvious thing to do but, if he did, the ambulance people would want to know why three children had been left in the house on their own. They would want to know who was supposed to be looking after them and where they were – and what could he say in reply? He could hardly tell them the truth.

The phone buzzed in his pocket, and, when he answered it, Emma told him that General Ghool wanted to know if it was all right to make himself a cup of tea. William said he would be right down.

'Wait here,' he told Amy, 'and keep an eye on Daniel.'

As he ran down the stairs and along the hall to his father's office, an idea was forming in his head. Maybe the General could be persuaded to pretend he was a relative of some sort, looking after the three of them while Mr and Mrs Seward were away. Then he could call an ambulance. He wasn't sure if it was polite to ask a star traveller if he'd mind doing this but it was the only idea he could think of.

He found the General in the kitchen, pouring

himself a large mug of tea and munching a sandwich. 'I hope you don't mind,' he said, 'but when I saw everything laid out, I presumed that . . .' He stopped and looked keenly at William. 'Is something wrong?'

'It's my brother,' said William. 'He's ill.'

'I'm sorry to hear that.' The General put down his sandwich. 'What is it?'

'I don't know,' said William, 'but his breathing's funny and he won't wake up properly.'

'Would you like me to take a look at him?' asked the General.

'Oh . . .' It had never occurred to William that General Ghool might be able to help directly. 'Are you . . . um . . .?'

'Everyone in the army has medical training these days,' said the General. 'I can handle most things.'

'Well, in that case, thank you,' said William. 'He's upstairs.'

Walking across the lobby to the lift, the General, still with his mug of tea in one hand, stopped to pull a box the size of a small suitcase from the wall. It had a large blue circle on the front, and William remembered seeing several of them at various points around the station.

'Medipac,' said the General briefly. 'You lead the way.'

In the bedroom, Daniel looked much the same, though he was now tossing and turning and muttering under his breath.

'He's not looking too good, is he?' The General put his mug down on the chest of drawers and came to stand by the bed.

'Will he be all right?' asked Amy.

'Oh, I think so.' General Ghool smiled re-assuringly as he placed the medipac on the floor. 'I've got just the thing in here to make him feel better. But I need some sugar. Could you get me some? From the kitchen?'

Amy turned and trotted off downstairs without a word.

'Do you know what's wrong?' asked William.

'At a guess I'd say it was blood poisoning,' said the General, 'but fortunately we don't have to rely on my guesses.' He opened the lid of the box and studied the contents for a moment. 'Have you ever used one of these?'

'No,' said William.

'Well, it's fairly simple. All you have to do is stick a couple of these on to the patient . . .' He took a flexible disc, about the size of a large coin, from a sterile pack and placed it carefully on Daniel's neck. Then he unpeeled another and lifted up Daniel's T-shirt to put it on his chest. '. . . And wait for the machine to give you a diagnosis. Has he cut himself recently, do you know?'

'He cut his hand,' said William, 'this morning.' He was about to ask how long it would take to get a diagnosis, when the box started talking.

'Diagnosis: septicaemia,' it said in a low, calm voice, very like Emma's. 'Treatment: apply patch to any free surface of skin immediately.' At the same time, there was a faint whirring noise and another sterile pack appeared in the top of the box with a blue circle flashing above it. General Ghool picked it up, peeled off the outer covering and slapped the disc on to Daniel's arm.

'There we go. That should sort him out!'

William noticed the difference almost immediately. His brother's breathing began to slow, the muscles in his neck relaxed and he looked calmer. A minute or so later, he was breathing normally, the colour had returned to his face and soon after that he was sleeping peacefully.

'No further treatment required,' said the box, 'but the patient is recommended to rest for eight hours.'

'You should get Larry to show you how to use these things one day. They can save a lot of worrying.' General Ghool closed the lid of the box. 'Ah, here she is! Thank you, my dear.'

Amy had come back with a bowl of sugar, and

the General took three spoonfuls and stirred them carefully into his tea. He lifted the cup to his lips and took a grateful sip. 'Oh, yes! Perfect!'

Amy was studying Daniel. 'Is he all right then?'

'He's fine,' said William. 'You can go back to sleep now.'

As Amy tucked herself back into the bottom bunk, he could feel the relief flooding through his body. It was only now the panic was over that he realized how frightened he had been.

'Thank you,' he said. 'I don't know what I'd have done if you hadn't –'

'Please!' The General held up a hand. 'Happy to help.' He picked up the medipac. 'Right. Back to base, I think!'

Downstairs, walking along the hall to the office, the General paused. 'I wonder,' he said, 'would it be possible to go outside for a moment?'

'Outside?' said William.

'Yes. I know it's not allowed, officially, but sometimes your father was kind enough to . . .'

William did not hesitate. If the General had wanted to take the family car and go nightclubbing William would have cheerfully handed over the keys after what he had done for Daniel.

'Of course,' he said.

He led General Ghool through to the sitting room, opened the doors to the patio and the

General stepped outside, took in a deep breath and stared out across the valley.

It was the middle of the night but it was not dark. There was a full moon and light flooded the sky. Its silvery colour gave varying shades of black and white to the fields that stretched down to the river and up the other side where it met the line of trees that ran along the ridge. The General seemed mesmerized by the view. Eventually, he turned to William with a sigh.

'You know, I must have been here . . . what, twenty, thirty times? But I've never seen this.'

'Seen what?' asked William.

'Moonlight,' said the General. 'Not many planets have it, you know. Your father always told me it was a very special sight and he was right. Quite extraordinary.'

William said nothing. He had never really thought of moonlight as extraordinary, or as anything except . . . moonlight, but if the General wanted to stand and look at it, that was fine with him.

'Thank you.' The General turned to smile at William. 'Now, I think I really must get back to those sandwiches.'

Back down in the station, General Ghool settled himself on a sofa in the sitting room with the plate of ham sandwiches on his lap.

'So what's all this about your parents going missing?' he asked between mouthfuls. 'Your father didn't say anything about leaving when I came through last Monday.'

'He didn't say anything to anyone,' said William, pouring out a fresh mug of tea. 'We just came home from school on Thursday and found he wasn't here. Mum had gone as well.'

The General frowned. 'They didn't leave a message? To say where they were going?'

'They didn't leave anything,' said William, and found himself describing how he and Daniel had eventually used the emergency phone, the arrival of Uncle Larry and then the astonishing discovery that his father was the manager of a Federation Star Portal.

The General listened to the story, munching solidly through the sandwiches as he did so, and only occasionally interrupting with a question.

'Most mysterious,' he said, as William ended by describing how Uncle Larry had gone to Byroid V because that was the only place his parents could be. 'But I'm sure he'll sort it out. Larry's not as stupid as he looks. Now . . .' The General put the sandwich plate on the table in front of him. 'Your father sometimes gave me something called *chocolate*. Would you happen to have . . . ?'

'Sure,' said William. 'No problem.' And it was while he was in the kitchen, getting a box of Black Magic from the stores, that Emma announced the return of Uncle Larry.

Uncle Larry came swooping up through the Portal and William could tell from his face that the news was not good.

'Complete failure,' he said, shaking his head in exasperation as he stepped over the side of the Portal. 'Not a trace of them anywhere. Nobody's heard anything, nobody's seen them . . .' He pulled on the robe William offered him. 'I can't understand it!' He led the way out to the main lobby and along to his bedroom. 'I've checked all the incomings, I've been through the computer records, I've spoken to everyone at the station . . . and there's nothing. Not a trace of them. The manager swears they haven't been through!'

Uncle Larry pushed open the door to his room and William followed him inside.

'Does that mean they didn't go to Byroid V after all?'

'They *must* have gone there!' Uncle Larry took his suit from the cupboard. 'There's nowhere else they could have gone, but if they did . . .' He forced his face into a smile. 'Don't worry, I'm sure we'll find them. It's just going to take a bit longer than I thought. How's everything been here? Bricks went through all right, did they?'

'They were fine,' said William.

'Any messages for me?' Uncle Larry was pulling on his shirt.

'The only message was the one saying General Ghool was going to arrive and –'

'General Ghool?' Uncle Larry froze. 'He's not supposed to be here for two days!'

'No,' said William, 'but he came early because –'

'Came?' Uncle Larry's voice went up a notch. 'You mean he's already here?'

'He got here about an hour ago. He's in the sitting room having a . . .' but William found he was speaking to an empty space. Still buttoning his trousers, Uncle Larry was already out the door.

'I am *so* sorry I wasn't here to meet you, General.' Uncle Larry pushed open the door to the sitting room. 'And I do apologize for there being no one here to look after you, but . . .' He stopped, taking in the General sitting on the sofa, his mug of tea in one hand and the last of the sandwiches in the other. 'Is . . . is everything all right?'

'Everything's fine with me,' said the General cheerfully. 'Have you found Jack and Lois yet?'

'Good . . . No . . . Well, I've been to Byroid V,'

Uncle Larry sat on the sofa opposite, his eyes still darting round to check that everything was as it should be, 'but there's no sign of them.'

'Ah.' The General nodded thoughtfully. 'So where are they?'

'I'm not sure,' said Uncle Larry, 'but we'll sort it out eventually . . . Have you got everything? I mean . . . is there anything you need?'

William appeared with the box of chocolates, which he placed on the table between the sofas.

'Don't worry about me,' said the General. 'I've been looked after very well.'

CHAPTER SIX

'So what happens next?' William asked Uncle Larry the following morning. 'About my parents?'

'Well, I've been thinking about that.' Uncle Larry was sitting in the kitchen with a large mug of tea, some of which he had already managed to spill down the front of his suit. 'And I think the next thing is for me to get back to Byroid V.' He stood up and walked over to the window. 'If your parents have gone through the Portals to another world, the sooner I catch up with them and find out why, the better.'

'You can do that, can you?' asked William. 'Catch up with them, I mean?'

'Oh, yes!' Uncle Larry nodded confidently. 'You can't travel round the Federation without leaving some sort of trace. I'll go to the next worlds down the line, you see, root around a bit . . . I'll find them all right!' He turned to William. 'The only snag is I can't look after things here while I'm doing it. Can you manage without me a bit longer?'

'You mean . . . do the bricks?'

'There'll be a couple of passengers to look after as well, but I'll run over the routine with you before I go.'

'It's Monday tomorrow,' said William. 'I'm supposed to be at school.'

'Yes . . .' Uncle Larry frowned. 'I'm afraid you'll have to miss that. But it's only a few days. I'll be back Wednesday. Wednesday evening at the latest.'

'Oh,' said William. 'OK.'

It didn't feel as if he had a great deal of choice.

'Good!' Uncle Larry smiled. 'Now, how about you have some breakfast and then join me in the station. We'll go over the details down there.' He marched briskly to the door, spilling tea on the floor as he went, but stopped in the doorway.

'By the way,' he said, 'thank you for looking after things last night. General Ghool is an important man in the Federation. I wouldn't like him to have got the impression that the Portal Service wasn't coping with a little crisis and . . . well, thank you.'

★

William had his breakfast, and went to make sure Daniel was all right before going down to Uncle Larry. He found his brother on the terrace outside the sitting room with Amy, busily feeding sticks into a fire he had lit in the base of the barbecue. Beside him on the ground was a ball of earth about the size of a large grapefruit.

'He's cooking a hedgehog,' said Amy when William appeared. 'You have to wrap it in clay first and then put it in a fire.'

'It says in the book that you cook it for a couple of hours, then when you peel off the clay all the spikes come off.' Daniel looked suspiciously at his brother. 'I suppose you've come to tell me I can't do it.'

'Well . . .' said William.

'Hedgehogs aren't poisonous!' protested Daniel. 'People have been eating them since forever.'

'Yes,' said William, 'but I just wondered if it was dead when you found it.'

Daniel looked at him. 'Why?'

'Because I remember Dad saying once that you should never eat anything without knowing how it died. If it had some disease, then you'd get it as well, wouldn't you?'

Daniel was still thinking about this when Mrs Duggan and Timber appeared. She came over to stand by William.

'Heard your brother was a bit poorly last night,' she said.

'Yes,' said William, 'but he's OK now.'

Mrs Duggan grunted. 'Your uncle around?'

'He's working,' said William. 'I could get him for you?'

'No need,' said Mrs Duggan. 'Only wanted to ask about my money.'

William remembered that Mrs Duggan usually came up to the house on a Saturday to receive her wages for the work she did on the farm. She had come up yesterday but, as there had been no Mrs Seward to give her the money, she had gone away again.

'I'll tell him,' he said. 'I'm sure he'll sort it out.'

Remembering the quantity of notes the old man had stuffed in his wallet, he thought there should be no problem finding enough to give her.

'No rush.' Mrs Duggan nodded in the direction of Daniel. 'What's he doing?'

'He's cooking a hedgehog,' said William.

'Don't let him eat it,' said Mrs Duggan, and William was about to promise that he wouldn't, when he realized Mrs Duggan had been talking to the dog.

'Money was one of the things I had to tell you about,' said Uncle Larry, when William told him about Mrs Duggan needing her wages. 'Any time you need any, it's in here.'

They were standing by the desk in the pantry, and Uncle Larry pulled open a drawer. It was filled to the brim with neat packets of ten, twenty and fifty pound notes. There had to be thousands, no, *hundreds* of thousands of pounds there, thought William.

'If I need any money . . . I take it?'

'Your dad always wrote down what he took in here.' Uncle Larry pointed to a battered notebook lying on top of the money with *Cash* written on the front. 'But the important thing is to make sure you let me know when you're running out. So I can organize getting some more.'

'More . . .' said William. 'Right . . .'

'And you probably ought to have a look at this if you have a moment.' Uncle Larry picked up a large grey book with no title on the front, and dropped it on the desk with a thump. 'It's the *Station Manager's Manual*. Tells you all the things you should and shouldn't do.'

William picked up the book. It was large and heavy. 'I have to read all this?'

'Technically, yes,' said Uncle Larry, 'as you're the temporary manager. But don't panic. Most of it's common sense. As long as you do the bricks, look after the passengers, and don't let anyone outside know about all this . . .' he gestured to the station around them, ' . . . you can't go far wrong. And if you're stuck you can always ask Emma.' He looked round the office. 'Now, what else do I have to show you?'

There were several things Uncle Larry had to show William. There were the translator pods, in case anyone came through the station without an implant and William couldn't understand what they were saying. There was the code for the storage seals on the food and drink cabinets, and there were the medipacs.

'I should have told you about these before,' said Uncle Larry, pulling the box off the wall in the central lobby. 'There's half a dozen of them scattered over the station and they're very easy to use.' He explained how the patches worked out what was wrong and sent the information back to the box so that it could provide a cure.

'It gets a bit more complicated if you've got an arm missing or you're bleeding to death,' he said, putting the medipac back on the wall and heading for the Portal, 'but the principle's still the same. You do whatever the box tells you. It's very clever. Even gives you a couple of options if your patient's already dead.'

Standing by the Portal he began taking off his suit. 'You've got the letter for Mrs Duggan?'

'Yes,' said William.

'Well, don't forget. If there's any problems, ask Emma to send me a message on the bricks. If it's an emergency, you can always send it to Brin on Q'vaar. He's only a station away and he can be with you in a blink.'

'OK,' said William.

'But you'll be fine, I know you will. And I'll be back on Wednesday.' Uncle Larry stepped on to the floor of the Portal in his shorts. 'And by then we'll have this whole business sorted out. One way or another.'

After he'd gone, William bent down to pick up the pile of clothes and took them through to the laundry, hoping as he did so that Uncle Larry was right.

He wanted very much for everything to be sorted out.

The envelope that William took down to Mrs Duggan contained her wages – Uncle Larry had put in a couple of extra twenty pound notes as a thank you for looking after William and Daniel the night their parents had 'gone on holiday' – and a letter to explain that William would not be going to school for the next three days.

Mrs Duggan read it carefully while sitting on the footplate of the tractor parked outside her cottage.

'Says here you're going to be off sick,' she said when she'd finished.

'Yes,' said William, 'but I won't really be ill. It's just that Uncle Larry needs me to help with his work for a few days.'

Mrs Duggan nodded, counted her money and tucked it carefully into a pocket of her dungarees before standing up.

'Thought I might ask you all to lunch,' she said.

'Lunch?'

Mrs Duggan gestured to the kitchen door. 'Got a chicken in the oven. Thought you might appreciate someone else doing the cooking.'

'Thank you,' said William. 'Yes, we would.'

Mrs Duggan's lunch, he realized later, was the first real meal he and Daniel had eaten since Mum and Dad had disappeared. Mrs Duggan had done proper vegetables and gravy to go with the roast chicken, and there was an apple pie and ice cream for afters. It tasted very good, and sitting round the table in the tiny kitchen was very warm and pleasant. When the meal was over, and Daniel and Amy had disappeared upstairs and Mrs Duggan said she had to get back to cleaning out the fuel line on the tractor, William found a part of himself didn't want to leave.

'Shame your uncle couldn't join us,' said Mrs Duggan as she walked him to the door.

'Yes,' William agreed. He couldn't say that Uncle Larry was by now on a planet nearly four light years away, so he had simply said that he was 'working' and couldn't come.

'Next time, eh?' said Mrs Duggan.

'Next time,' William agreed. He thanked her again for the lunch, and set off back up the track to the farmhouse.

As he left, he heard Mrs Duggan quietly asking Timber to get her a screwdriver – a flathead this time, not a Phillips.

The farmhouse, when he got back, seemed empty and cold. He thought of doing his homework but, as he wasn't going into school on Monday, decided there wasn't much point and sat on a sunlounger on the terrace instead, trying to read the *Station Manager's Manual*.

Looking out over the valley, he realized that he was worried about his parents in a way that he hadn't been since the day he and Daniel had come home to find them gone. Somehow, Uncle Larry had always made it seem that finding them was just a minor inconvenience that would soon be sorted out – annoying but not the sort of thing to cause any real anxiety. Now, he wasn't so sure. The feeling was growing inside him that whatever had happened was more serious than Uncle Larry was letting on.

The house still felt empty, even when Daniel came home at six o'clock for supper. Not that Daniel himself seemed to notice. Mrs Duggan had given him the feet of the chicken they had eaten and he sat at the kitchen table, picking open the muscles with a knife and sorting out which ones you had to pull to make the toes move. Then, when he'd finished with that, he began cleaning the hedgehog's skull with the sharpened end of a matchstick.

As the evening wore on, William found he was becoming more worried rather than less and he was quite glad, after doing the bricks at a quarter to nine, when it was time for bed. For some reason, the words Larry had spoken as he left kept repeating themselves in his head.

'I'll be back on Wednesday,' he had said, 'And by then we'll have this whole business sorted out. One way or another.'

It was that phrase 'one way or another' that bothered him.

CHAPTER SEVEN

The next morning William was too busy to do much worrying. There were the bricks at a quarter past seven – he had set three alarm clocks to make sure he woke up in time. There was Daniel to wake up and get ready for school – he thought he should be allowed to stay home as well, but William persuaded him that it wasn't fair to let Amy go on her own. And there were all the preparations for the passenger who would be arriving that morning – towels and soap to lay out, food to prepare, and cleaning machines to order into action.

The passenger was a round, cheerful-looking man called Hippo White. William had no idea if that was his real name or a translation of it, but Emma said he was a trader who made his living buying items in one part of the Federation and selling them in another. Dressed in a blue tunic and a pair of soft, baggy trousers that tucked into his boots, he came shooting up through the Portal a little after nine.

'Hi there! You must be William!' He held out a hand in greeting as he stepped over the lip of the Portal. 'Any news of your parents yet?'

'Not yet,' said William.

'I must say, it all sounds very odd.' Hippo followed William out to the lobby, pulling a small suitcase behind him. 'Brin was telling me about it. Where've they gone, do you think?'

'I don't know,' said William.

'Well, not to worry. Larry'll track them down.' Hippo paused in the lobby and looked round. 'Am I in the green suite?'

'Yes,' said William. 'If you'd like to follow me . . .'

'It's all right, I know the way!' Hippo was already striding towards the door. 'But if you could manage a pot of . . . um . . . what's it called . . .'

'Tea?' suggested William.

'That's the one!' said Hippo, and he disappeared into his room.

William made a pot of tea and took it, with a plate of sandwiches, across to the green suite. Inside, Hippo was dictating a series of messages to Emma that he wanted sending out with the next brick and he gestured to William to leave the tray on the table.

William did as he was told and went back to sit in the pantry. He opened the *Station Manager's Manual* and settled down to read the chapter on 'Defence of the Station: The Use of Small Arms', which gave all the rules prescribing how and when it was permissible to use which weapons from the armoury. He was still reading – and making the occasional trip to the weapons room so that Emma could show him which guns the book was talking about – when Hippo finally emerged from his room nearly three hours later.

'Your father didn't leave anything for me, did he?' he asked as he walked round to the pantry and peered inside. 'Flat . . . round . . . about this big?'

'Dad didn't leave anything for anybody,' said William. 'He just disappeared.' Then, seeing the look of disappointment on Hippo's face, he added, 'Was it something important?'

'Well, it was quite.' Hippo thrust his hands in his pockets. 'He was making something for me, and he said he'd have it ready for the next time I came through. Byroid's the big market you see. That's where I need it for.'

'Oh,' said William.

'Have you checked his workshop?' asked Hippo. 'I mean, do you know if he had a chance to finish it?'

'Dad had a workshop?' said William.

'Oh, yes! Down there!' Hippo pointed to the stairs in the centre of the lobby.

William had not explored the lower level of the station yet. Uncle Larry had told him there was nothing down there of any importance. 'If I knew where the workshop was, I could look,' he said, 'but . . .'

'I know where it is!' Hippo was already heading for the stairs. 'Let me show you!'

Lights came on automatically as they descended the spiral staircase and, at the bottom, William found himself in an area almost identical to the floor above, though with seven doors leading from the lobby instead of nine.

'This is where the Old Portal used to be,' said Hippo, gesturing vaguely around him as he marched purposefully to a door on the right, 'and your dad's workshop is in here.'

William followed him into a room that was about the same size as the kitchen on the floor above. Workbenches ran along the walls, there was a row of cupboards at the far end and, in the centre of the room, a large table contained a variety of strange objects, most of them in pieces.

Halfway down the workbench on the right was a battered swivel chair, with photos pinned to the wall in front of it. As William looked at one of them, the image of his mother smiled and waved back at him.

'Found it!' Hippo was standing at the table holding up a flat disc about half a metre in diameter. When he let go, it floated gently down and then hovered a few centimetres above the floor. 'And it looks as if your father's worked his usual magic!'

'What is it?' asked William.

'Grav-sled,' said Hippo. 'Any chance we could try it outside?'

The idea of a grav-sled, William discovered, was that you stood on it, leaned in a particular direction, and the grav-sled took you there. Quite fast.

'They were *the* way to get to work a couple of years back,' said Hippo, stepping carefully on to the disc as it floated above the ground outside the back door. 'They sold thousands of them until the accidents.' His face clouded for a moment. 'Sales sort of petered out after that, but your dad reckoned he could put in a modified Tenebrian force field and the thing would be perfectly safe.' He balanced on the disc for a moment. 'So, let's give it a try . . .'

He leaned to one side and the sled began moving down towards the barn, rapidly gathering speed as it went. By the time it hit the side of the barn, William thought, it was going fast enough for Hippo to kill himself, but nothing happened – to Hippo or to the side of the barn. Instead, something cushioned its stop and a quite unharmed Hippo waved cheerily back at William.

'Seems to work,' he shouted. 'Didn't feel a thing!'

For nearly half an hour, Hippo flung the gravsled around the sky with an ever increasing confidence. He ran it into walls and trees, he tried looping the loop to see if he could fall off and he flew the sled around the house and across the fields with an awesome speed.

'That is *excellent!*' he said, a little breathlessly, when he finally came to a halt. 'Couldn't be better. Want to give it a try?'

William gave it a try. He moved a little more cautiously than Hippo, and it was a while before he got the knack of how far to lean and for how long, but after a few trips round the house and down the valley to the river he had to admit that it was seriously good fun.

'Let's hope they agree with you on Byroid,' said Hippo, 'because if they do I'm going to be a very rich man. Now,' he tucked the disc under his arm, 'the one thing we need to do before I go is find out how much I owe your dad and settle up.'

William looked rather blank.

'It'll be in the book in his workshop,' said Hippo confidently. 'Your dad always wrote everything down.'

The two of them returned to the station and, sure enough, lying on the desk in the workshop, William found a large blue notebook. *Item 639,* said his father's careful hand-writing, was *Hippo's grav-sled,* and there followed a list of the things he had done to it. At the end, under the heading *Cost,* were the words *No charge.*

'It says there's no charge,' said William.

'That sounds like your dad all right,' said Hippo. 'I keep telling him he ought to make people pay for what he does, but he says he enjoys it too much to . . .' He stopped. 'Are you all right?'

William had gone very pale. He had just noticed the time and date of his father's last entry. Alterations to the sled, it said, had been completed at two o'clock in the afternoon of 17 July. That was the day he and Mum had disappeared, and two o'clock was almost exactly two hours before William and Daniel had come home and found the house empty.

At two o'clock, his father had carefully made a note of what he'd done in the workshop and then

. . . and then what? It made no sense. None of it made any sense at all.

'I'll tell you one thing,' said Hippo, 'and I say this as someone who's known your dad for a good many years . . .' He was standing in the green suite, packing the grav-sled into his case while William watched from the door. 'Wherever your dad's gone, he'll have had a very good reason for going there.'

William nodded politely. He wanted to believe it was true, but it wasn't easy. Why should Dad have left without leaving a word? Left just an hour or two after he was writing in a notebook that he had finished rebuilding the sled? How could anyone disappear for five days without saying where they were going?

'Not only will he have had a good reason,' said Hippo firmly, 'but I'm quite sure he'll be back, *with* your mother and, when he is, I want you to tell him how grateful I am for his fixing the sled and give him this as a little thank-you present.'

'What is it?' asked William. The object Hippo had passed him looked rather like a torch.

'It's a torch,' said Hippo. 'Got all the usual gadgets – wide beam, infra-red, low-glo and so on, but it also lights up anyone who's wearing a shield.'

'Oh,' said William.

'You don't know what a shield is, do you?' said Hippo.

'No,' said William.

'Well, it's a very useful device that –'

'The Portal is now ready,' Emma's voice interrupted from the ceiling. 'Departure time is set for sixty seconds.'

'You'd better get Emma to tell you.' Hippo picked up his case and headed for the door. 'And don't worry about your father! Like I said, there'll be a perfectly simple explanation for where he's gone. Send me a message when he gets back, will you? Emma's got the address.'

'OK,' said William, and after he had watched the trader disappear through the Portal, he tried very hard to believe what Hippo had told him.

That there was no need to worry.

That there was a perfectly simple explanation for everything that had happened.

And that all he had to do was wait until Uncle Larry came back and told him what it was.

CHAPTER EIGHT

At four o'clock, when Daniel got back from school, William had tea ready for him in the kitchen, with bread and butter on the table and eggs boiling in the pan. He had the idea that, if things were as normal as possible, it might help his brother not to worry about what had happened to their parents and why they had apparently been left to look after themselves.

Not that Daniel looked worried – except possibly by the fact that he had to go to school while William stayed at home. After wolfing down his tea, he went straight outside and sat happily on the back step to dissect the body of a dead mole he had found on the playing field at school.

He looked as if he hadn't a care in the world, thought William, and he realized with a start that his brother had never once asked why their parents had left so suddenly or when they might get back. Daniel seemed able to accept everything that had happened and simply get on with life – and William rather envied him.

At half past five, he went down to the station to do the bricks and found there was a message for him from Brin, the station manager on Q'Vaar.

'Hi there!' The burly, bearded figure was displayed this time above the desk in the pantry. 'Larry tells me you're looking after the station on your own until Wednesday, and I just wondered if you wanted a hand. I can come right over if you do. Let me know, eh?'

William briefly considered accepting this offer, but decided in the end to say no. There was another passenger due the next day but he thought he could manage her quite easily on his own, so he recorded a message for Emma to send out with the next bricks, saying thank you, but he was fine.

Back upstairs, he found Daniel sitting at the kitchen table with a straw.

'I've got to do a "How it Works" in class on Wednesday and I thought I'd do lungs,' he explained, when William asked what he was doing. He blew through the straw and the tiny viscous sacs he had taken from the mole inflated on the table. 'What do you think?'

William remembered Daniel's teacher as a small, nervous woman who was frightened of spiders.

'Looks like a winner to me,' he said. 'Go for it.'

The bricks came through at 3.49 a.m. and afterwards, when William went back to bed, he found it difficult to sleep. It was nearly seven before he finally nodded off and the alarm rang twenty minutes later to wake him up to get Daniel ready for school. After his brother had left, he thought of going back to bed, but instead went down to the station to check that all was ready for his second passenger when she arrived that afternoon.

Checking everything was ready took most of the morning, but this was mainly because, halfway through it, William found the torch that Hippo had left on the desk in his room and asked Emma what the trader had meant when he said that it 'lit up' shields.

'A shield,' Emma explained, 'is a device that renders the carrier invisible to the normal bandwidth of radiation. Shining the torch on them, however, will give a reflection that enables you to see them.'

What this meant was that if you were carrying a 'shield' you were invisible, but that if someone shone the torch at you, they could still see where you were. Intriguingly, it turned out that there were several 'shields' in one of the drawers of his father's desk in the pantry. They were green, egg-shaped objects, rattling around amongst the pens, the paperclips and a roll of sticky tape – and when you held one in your hand you became invisible.

William thought the shields were more interesting than the torch, and he took one upstairs so that he could try it outside. Even though there was no one around, it was an oddly exciting sensation to walk through the farmyard knowing that he couldn't be seen. Birds flew round and ignored him and he got close enough to a pigeon on the ground to touch its back.

Daniel, he thought, would kill to get his hands on one of these.

Mrs Hepworth, William's second passenger, was supposed to arrive at three o'clock that afternoon, but a message with the bricks that arrived shortly after two said she had been delayed and would not be arriving until ten o'clock that night.

When she did arrive, it was not a happy visit. She was a tall, elderly woman and almost the first thing she asked was that William take her outside.

'I know it's night-time,' she said, 'but you've probably got some night goggles around the place, haven't you? I'm particularly anxious to see an owl.'

William, however, had been reading the *Station Manager's Manual* that afternoon and discovered that it was strictly against the rules for any passenger through the Portal to leave the station and go outside. Why no one had mentioned this before he did not know, but the manual was very definite that, on a restricted planet, nothing must be allowed to give even the slightest hint of the existence of the Federation. Anyone allowing this to happen was liable to the severest penalties.

'You're saying I can't go out at all?' said Mrs Hepworth.

'I'm sorry,' said William, 'but those are the rules.'

'Well, in that case I suppose I have no choice, do I?' Mrs Hepworth gave a sniff and walked through to the sitting room, clearly very angry.

William called in occasionally during the next six hours to ask if she wanted anything to eat or drink but the answer was always the same. Mrs Hepworth did not want anything and simply sat, staring out at the picture of the night sky through the windows until it was time for her to leave, still visibly upset. William was upset as well. He had enjoyed meeting General Ghool and Hippo White and now . . .

Now he was mostly very tired. When Mrs Hepworth left at four in the morning, he was finding it difficult to keep himself awake, and he had just finished clearing up and was about to go upstairs to bed when Emma informed him that an emergency brick had arrived with a request from the medical centre on Riga that he stand by the Portal until further notice.

It seemed there had been an outbreak of plague on Tychel – a mutation of a dangerous bog virus – and the medical researchers on Riga were working round the clock to find a cure. When they did, it would need to be sent to Tychel as fast as possible and all station managers were asked to stand by their Portals, ready to send it on the instant it arrived. This was one of those occasions when even seconds might count.

There was no indication of how long William would have to wait, though Emma said it was unlikely to be longer than six or seven hours. If the cure didn't come before then, she said, the people on Tychel would all be dead anyway. In fact, the cure came through shortly before seven and William sent it safely on its way. After that, it was time to go upstairs, wake Daniel and send him off to school with his packed lunch – making sure it was in a separate box from the one with the mole's lungs.

Ten minutes later, as William was climbing gratefully under the bedclothes, the front doorbell rang.

'Morning!' said a cheery-looking man in green overalls when William opened the door. 'Patio doors.' He gestured with his thumb to the van behind him where another man was already unloading pieces of white plastic. 'Is your dad in?'

William hesitated. 'Dad's working.'

'Well, if you could let him know we're here,' said the man, 'then we'll get started.'

'You . . . you're going to fit them now?'

'That's the plan.' The man smiled happily. 'Any chance of a cup of tea?'

'Oh,' said William. 'Right.'

'One with sugar and one without,' said the man and then added, as William turned to go, 'No school today then?'

'I'm off sick,' said William.

'Yeah . . .' The man looked at him. 'You don't look too good. You should take it easy.'

'Thank you,' said William. 'I'll try.'

The next bricks arrived at 10.32 a.m. and brought another message from Brin on Q'Vaar.

'How are you managing?' asked the figure in the hologram. 'I know you've had a busy night but are you all right? Let me know, will you?'

William was about to record a reply for Emma to attach to the next bricks when the station computer informed him the workmen were looking for him upstairs.

The man fitting the patio doors wanted to know if the fascia board should overlap the bricks or not. William had no idea what a fascia board was.

'What do you think would be best?' he asked.

'Well, if it was me,' said the workman, 'I'd have it like this.' He held up a piece of plastic against the brick. 'But you're paying. It's your choice.'

'Let's have it like that,' said William.

'You're sure?'

'Positive,' said William.

And it went on like that all day. As the hours passed, William found it harder and harder to stay awake and by four o'clock, when Daniel got back from school, he was so tired it was getting difficult to understand what people were saying.

'Mrs Catterall fainted when I showed her my lungs,' said Daniel, throwing his bag on the floor, 'and two people were sick. There's a van outside. What's going on?'

William explained about the new patio doors and Daniel asked if he could have the old ones so he could break all the glass in them with a hammer. William was still trying to work out the best way of saying no when the phone in his pocket vibrated.

'You have a passenger arriving shortly,' Emma told him.

It took a moment for the news to penetrate through the fog in William's brain. A passenger? Another one? Without any warning?

'How shortly?' he asked.

'Arrival expected in two minutes,' said Emma.

Moving hurriedly down the hall to his father's office, William wondered who it could be. Perhaps it was Uncle Larry, coming back earlier than expected with news. Perhaps, he thought briefly, it was his parents . . .

But the figure that came up through the Portal was not Uncle Larry, nor was it his parents. It was a short man with a head of dark curly hair and a big black beard that William was sure he had seen before but couldn't remember where.

'Sorry to arrive out of the blue like this,' the man said as he stepped out of the Portal, 'but I really was quite worried. And when you didn't answer my message this morning, I thought I'd better come over.'

William suddenly remembered who the man was. It was Brin, the station manager from Q'Vaar.

'I . . . I'm fine. Thank you.'

'Really?' Brin looked at him closely. 'How much sleep have you had in the last two days?'

William tried to think. There had been a few

hours before the bricks arrived on Tuesday . . . or was it Monday? What day was it today? He struggled to remember . . .

'I thought so.' Brin placed a stubby hand on William's shoulder and led him towards the lift. 'Come on, you're going to bed.'

'I can't yet,' William insisted. 'There's men doing the doors and I've got to make sure Daniel doesn't . . .'

'I'll look after Daniel,' said Brin firmly. 'Bed. Now.'

CHAPTER NINE

The following morning, after more than twelve hours sleep, William was feeling a lot better. He came down to the kitchen to find the station manager from Q'Vaar standing at the sink, vigorously cleaning the taps.

'Hi there!' Brin gave him a cheery smile. 'How're you feeling?'

'Fine, thanks,' said William. 'I'm sorry about . . .'

'Not your fault at all,' said Brin briskly. 'Larry should never have left you to manage on your own. Running a station is not a one-man job. He knows that as well as I do. When things start piling up, or you fall ill, or there's an emergency, you have to have two people on a station. You have to!'

'Yes,' said William. 'I was wondering if my brother . . .'

'Nothing to worry about there,' said Brin reassuringly. 'All under control. I gave him breakfast and Larry took him down to the bus.'

'Uncle Larry's here?'

'Got in last night,' said Brin. 'And I told him! Leaving one person in charge of a station is asking for trouble, I said. Especially when that person is —'

'Did he find my parents?' interrupted William. 'Does he know where they went?'

'Ah . . . no . . . well . . .' Brin put down his cloth and turned to face William. 'It's not good news there, I'm afraid.'

'Why? What's happened?'

'Nothing. Well, nothing we know of . . .' Brin looked slightly embarrassed. 'Larry doesn't have any news about your parents, because he didn't find them.'

'But he said he would!' William was puzzled. 'He said there had to be a trace!'

'Yes, well, he can explain that one to you himself.' Brin dried his hands and crossed the kitchen. 'He said to bring you down as soon as you were awake. Come on!'

Uncle Larry was in the pantry down at the station, dictating a report to Emma. His face lit up when he saw William, but beneath the smile, William thought, he looked both tired and worried.

'Brin's right,' he said. 'I didn't find any news of your parents. I've been up and down both the other lines out of Byroid V and there wasn't even a whisper. It's like they were never there.'

'But you said it was the only place they could have gone –'

'I did.' Uncle Larry nodded his agreement. 'And I still can't understand it. There was only a very narrow window in which they could have travelled, you see. The Portal at Byroid V was down for six hours that day. You saw them before you went to school, they weren't here when you got back, so the only time they could have gone anywhere was between about eight o'clock and ten. You'd have thought with only two hours to check –'

'No,' said William. 'No, they can't.'

Uncle Larry frowned. 'Can't what?'

'They can't have gone in the morning,' said William, 'because they were still here then. At least Dad was.'

He told Uncle Larry about the entry he had found in his father's logbook down in the workshop. Uncle Larry wanted to see it for himself and they all went down to look.

Sitting in the swivel chair at the workbench, Uncle Larry stared at the entry on the page for some time without speaking. 'If this is genuine,' he said eventually, 'then they can't have gone through the Portal at all.' He looked thoughtfully at Brin. 'And you must be right.'

'Right about what?' asked William.

'Brin thinks your parents might have gone on a little trip. Out beyond the farm.'

'I thought you said if they'd gone anywhere outside the farm, Emma would know?'

'Normally that would be true,' said Brin, 'but your dad was very clever with machinery.' He gestured round the workshop. 'It was his hobby. I reckon, if he wanted to override the fence circuit, he was smart enough to do it.'

'But why would he want to?'

Uncle Larry gave a shrug.

'Station managers sometimes get fed up with having to stay in one place all the time,' said Brin. 'Maybe your parents decided to go out for a meal together, or take a trip to the cinema –'

'The cinema?' protested William. 'They've been gone nearly a week!'

'The possibility Brin has in mind . . .' Uncle Larry was thoughtfully examining his fingernails. ' . . . is that, while they were out there, they had some sort of . . . accident.'

An accident! William wondered why he hadn't thought of it before. Of course. They could have gone out for a walk, been hit by a car, taken to hospital . . .

'Should we call the police?' he asked.

'Can't tell the police,' said Brin firmly. 'Far too risky.'

'But –'

'I'm afraid Brin's right,' said Uncle Larry. 'We can't afford to have the police involved but, fortunately, that's not the only way to find out what happened. I'll send a dispatch to the Admiral in charge of the Federation Security Forces that ensure this planet's isolation. They'll look into it for us. And I promise you, if anything happened out there to your parents, they'll find out about it.'

'They're very thorough,' said Brin. 'And if your parents were using shields or anything, the FSF have got the technology to track them down.'

'How long will it take?'

'Depends,' said Uncle Larry. 'A few days, perhaps a week.'

'Which leaves us the question of what to do about William while they're looking,' said Brin. 'Because you can't leave him to manage the station on his own. He needs someone to help him and you can't –'

'Yes, all right!' Uncle Larry interrupted rather testily. 'I think you've made your point on that one.'

★

When Uncle Larry went off to meet with Federation Security – he disappeared, quite literally, into thin air somewhere over the front lawn – Brin and William went back down to the station.

'I thought I'd go over some of the duties of a station manager,' said Brin, 'in case Larry missed anything out.' And for the next three hours he gave William detailed instructions on the care and maintenance of a Star Portal.

Brin's instructions were nothing like the advice Uncle Larry had given. There were no vague statements of how it was 'mostly common sense' or how, if there was a problem, he should 'ask Emma'. According to Brin, there were very definite rules about how passengers should be treated, when and how you should talk to them, rules about what food they should be offered and a lot of rules about hygiene and cleaning. Brin was very big on cleaning.

While they worked, he also gave William a brief history of the Portals and the Federation. He told him how the first human civilizations had spread, in great colony ships that floated between the stars for generations, in their search for new worlds. He told him how the process had speeded up when the first Star Portals had been built, even though they could only transport people at the speed of light – and then of the discovery of time-tunnel technology and the gates that could send you to another world in an instant.

'That's when the Federation was really born,' he said. 'You couldn't have a Federation without the Portals and, as we're the people who keep the Portals open, your dad always said it meant we have one of the most important jobs in the world. Not that the passengers know that!' He chuckled. 'You get some right oddballs coming through, I can tell you!'

That was when William told him about Mrs Hepworth and how upset she had been when he told her she couldn't go outside.

'You didn't let her outside?' Brin looked puzzled. 'Why not?'

'It says in the manual I'm not allowed to,' said William, 'because we're a restricted planet.'

'Ah . . .' Brin smiled. 'I'm afraid that's one of the rules that everyone bends a little. As long as there's no chance of it leading to someone finding out about the station, there's no harm in taking people out for a walk – that's what all the clothes are for.'

'Clothes?'

'In the wardrobe room.' Brin gestured across the lobby. 'Passengers would look a bit odd outside in their own clothes, so your dad kept something for most sizes and seasons.'

'I'm not surprised Mrs Hepworth was so upset,'

he went on. 'You have to try and imagine what it's like to come to another world, a different planet, that most people in the Federation aren't allowed to visit, and have a chance to walk on it, breathe the air . . . You may be used to it, but to a visitor it's more special than you might think.'

William thought of General Ghool looking out over the valley in the moonlight.

'So I can let them out whenever they want?'

'Your dad never let passengers out on their own,' said Brin. 'Your mother usually went with them. Partly to keep an eye on them and partly because she was the one who could answer any questions they might have. About plants and animals and that sort of thing.'

Brin paused. 'He was going to tell you about all this, you know. This summer. He reckoned you'd be old enough, and he was going to show you the station, maybe let you start helping look after things, meet a few passengers . . .'

'But then he disappeared,' said William.

'Yes,' said Brin. 'I don't understand that any more than you do.' He placed a hand comfortingly on William's shoulder. 'But maybe Larry'll pick up some clues today, eh?'

They did pick up one clue about what had happened to William's parents that day, but it was not as a result of anything Uncle Larry discovered from the Federation Security Forces. The information came from Mr Drew, the vet, who arrived at the back door at lunchtime, accompanied by a slightly breathless Mrs Duggan and Timber.

'Ah, William.' Mr Drew had called in many times over the last few years and knew him well. 'Are your parents around?'

'They're away at the moment,' said William. 'Is anything wrong?'

'I'm not sure.' Mr Drew held up a large leather bag. 'I found this in the quarry. It's your mother's, isn't it?'

'Yes!' William recognized the bag at once. It was the one his mother took whenever she went out for a walk. It carried a bottle of water, her notebooks and any plant specimens she might find on the way.

'I was a little concerned . . .' The vet placed the bag carefully on the table. 'Because these spots here . . .' he pointed to one corner of the bag, '. . . are blood.' He looked across at William. 'Is everything all right?'

CHAPTER TEN

'Blood?' said William. 'Are you sure?'

'Positive,' said the vet. 'Where is your mother at the moment?'

'She's . . . she's gone on holiday.' William reached forward to touch the bag. 'Where did you say you found it?'

'The quarry,' said Mr Drew.

'Called him out cos of one of the sheep,' said Mrs Duggan. 'Fell over the edge.'

William knew the quarry. It was a large hole dug in the side of the hill on the edge of the farm and used now as a rubbish dump. If a sheep had fallen into it, he was not surprised it had been injured. There were all sorts of rusted bits of metal down there.

'I saw the bag,' it was Mr Drew speaking again,

'when I climbed down to the sheep. And there was more blood on the ground. You say your mother's gone on holiday?'

'Yes.'

'When did she go?'

William was finding it hard to think. It was his mother's bag – she never went anywhere without it – and now it had been found in the quarry. With blood on it.

'William?' repeated the vet. 'When did she go?'

'Last . . . last Thursday, I think.'

'Thursday?' Mr Drew frowned. 'I was out here Thursday morning, and your mother didn't say anything about going on holiday. Where's she gone?'

'France,' said William. 'She went with Dad.'

'Do you know where in France?'

'Not really. They're camping.'

'Postcard came,' said Mrs Duggan. 'On the Saturday.' She pointed at the card on the dresser.

The vet picked it up and read it. 'They went for a surprise holiday on the Thursday and you got this card on the Saturday?'

William nodded.

'I'm sorry,' said Mr Drew, 'but there's something not quite right about all this. I think it might be best if we call the police.'

'The police?'

'I don't wish to alarm you . . .' Mr Drew reached into his pocket and took out his mobile. 'But it seems clear to me that there's been some sort of accident. The bag, the blood, your parents not being here – I could be wrong but I think –'

Mr Drew never got to say what he thought, because at that moment Mrs Duggan hit him on the back of his head with a frying pan. It was a large, heavy pan and he fell to the floor with a quiet sigh of surprise. For a moment, nobody moved, except Timber, who picked up one of the chair cushions, lifted up the vet's head with his nose and pushed the cushion underneath with his paws.

'Brin still here?' asked Mrs Duggan.

'I . . . um . . . yes . . .' said William.

'Better go down and get him then,' said Mrs Duggan grimly. 'And tell him to bring a medipac.'

As William went racing along to the hall, he was thinking *down* . . . Mrs Duggan had told him to go down and get Brin. Which meant she knew about the station. She must have known all along. He found Brin in the recreation room, and told him what had happened. Before he was halfway through the story, Brin had grabbed the medipac and was running towards the lift.

In the kitchen, he gave Mrs Duggan a brief nod

and bent down beside the body on the floor. He took two discs from the medipac, stuck one on the vet's arm and the other on his neck.

'He was going to call the police,' said Mrs Duggan, peering anxiously down at the body. 'Didn't hit him too hard, did I?'

'Diagnosis: contusion to the back of the skull. Mild concussion probable,' said the voice from the medipac. 'Medication prepared.'

'He's fine.' Brin took a blue disc from the case and peeled off the cover. 'Big bruise, but most of that'll be gone by the time he wakes up.'

'Might be best,' said Mrs Duggan, 'if he didn't remember any of this.'

'I agree.' Brin burrowed in the medipac for a moment and came out with an orange-coloured device about the size of a bar of chocolate. 'How long do we need?'

Mrs Duggan looked up at the kitchen clock. 'He got here about two. Took us ten minutes to get to the quarry . . .' She paused for a moment. 'Couldn't be more'n half an hour.'

'I'll give him forty minutes,' said Brin, 'to be on the safe side.' He tapped at some keys on the device before placing it under the vet's head. He pointed to the bag. 'Could someone get rid of that before he comes round?'

Timber put his paws on the table, took the bag

in his teeth and carried it over to the kitchen dresser. Pushing open a door with his nose, he put the bag inside on a shelf and closed it again.

'Could someone tell me what's going on?' asked William. The speed with which everything was happening made him feel a bit as if he'd been hit on the head with a frying pan himself.

'I'm wiping out any memories he has of the last forty minutes,' said Brin, removing the device and then peeling off the patches he had placed on the vet. 'So when he comes round he won't remember anything about the bag or being hit on the head. We'll tell him . . .' He paused.

'Tell him he came up to the house to say hello,' said Mrs Duggan, 'and slipped on the floor.'

'Right.' Brin nodded. 'We don't need to make it any more complicated than that. It'll only confuse him.'

He wouldn't be the only one, thought William, and he watched as the vet gave a low groan and sat up.

'What . . . what happened?' he asked.

'You slipped,' said Brin.

'Tripped over that bit of carpet,' said Mrs Duggan. 'Banged your head. You all right?'

'I . . . I think so . . .' Mr Drew looked uncertainly round the kitchen. 'You . . . you wanted me to look at one of the sheep . . . didn't you?'

'No, no, you've done all that.' Mrs Duggan took him by the arm. 'Then we came up here to say hello to William, remember?'

'No . . .' said Mr Drew. 'No, I don't.'

'Bang on the head must have shaken you up pretty bad.' Mrs Duggan took him by the arm and steered him towards a chair.

'You sit yourself down,' said Brin, 'and I'll make a cup of tea.'

'Oh . . . That would be . . . Thank you.' Still looking rather dazed, Mr Drew did as he was told and smiled faintly at William. 'Hello, William! How are things with you?'

'Oh, fine,' said William. 'Couldn't be better.'

When Uncle Larry got back and heard what had happened, he looked at the bag with the blood and pulled thoughtfully at his beard. 'This whole business,' he said, 'gets more and more confusing.'

'Is it Mum's blood?' asked William. 'On the bag?'

'Yes,' said Uncle Larry, 'I think it is.'

'What do you think's happened? Has she had an accident?'

Uncle Larry did not answer directly. Instead, he stood up and walked over to the window, staring out at the fields at the back of the farmhouse.

'You know what bothers me?' he said eventually.

'You know what really bothers me about all this? It's that none of it makes any sense. None of it! I keep running through the possibilities in my head and none of them work!' He turned to William. 'You ask if your mother's had an accident. Well, let's imagine she did. Let's imagine she fell into the quarry and was so badly hurt she couldn't use her phone to call for help. But then what happened to your dad? Did he have an accident as well? At the same time? And even if that is what happened, where are the bodies?'

Uncle Larry began pacing up and down the kitchen.

'So maybe it wasn't an accident. Maybe it was a kidnapping. Maybe some terrorist pod from Pastinare is staging one of their protests against the Federation, but if it was, why haven't they said something? The whole point of a kidnapping is to make the other side give in to your demands, and nobody's made any demands.'

'Do you think they're dead?' asked William.

Uncle Larry stopped pacing, and turned to face him. 'Let's say they are,' he said. 'Let's take the worst case scenario and imagine both your parents have been murdered. They were very unlucky and they happen to have strayed into the path of a psychopath who murdered them both for no other reason than that's what he liked doing. But if that is what happened – and it means leaving aside the fact that your dad always carried a wham-gun and that either of them only had to press a button on their phones to raise the alarm – where are the bodies? If they were buried anywhere on the farm, Emma would know, and if they'd been taken outside the perimeter she'd know that as well. You see what I mean? It doesn't make sense! None of it makes any sense at all!'

'So we leave it to Federation Security to solve?' asked Brin.

Uncle Larry looked at him. 'I don't know what else we can do.' He picked up the bag. 'I'll give them this, tell them about the quarry and the blood, and ask them to get back to us as soon as they can.' He held up a hand as Brin opened his mouth to speak. 'And, yes, I know William can't manage the station on his own while we're waiting.' He sighed. 'I'm still working on that one.'

That night, as William lay in bed, thoughts of accidents, murder and kidnapping whirled through his mind. Something terrible had happened to his parents. That was why they had disappeared. That was why they were never going to come back. They had been attacked by an axe murderer, or run over by a bus or . . . or . . .

Thinking of all the things that might have

happened kept him awake a good deal of the night. He lay in bed, tossing and turning, trying to fight back a rising sense of panic, and only finally fell asleep towards dawn.

And while he slept, he had a dream.

He was on a ship, in a terrible storm. He was in a room below decks with a lot of other people, including Daniel and Amy and Mrs Duggan, and the ship was being thrown around by the waves and everyone was terrified that at any moment it would sink and they would all be drowned.

Someone should go up on deck, William thought, and find out what was happening. Were the waves big enough to overwhelm them? Were they near a shore and about to be thrown on the rocks? He needed to know, so, in the dream, he made his way up to the deck, then along a gangway through the howling wind and driving rain, and up a ladder that led to the bridge.

Pushing open the door, he was astonished to see the man at the helm was his father. His feet were braced against the deck, his arms gripped the wheel and his face peered out at the wind-torn waves ahead. William's mother was standing beside him and, when the wheel gave a lurch to the right, she reached out to help steady it.

William's heart filled at the sight of them. He wanted to rush over and hug them, to tell them how much he had missed them and how worried he had been, but he knew at once that they shouldn't be disturbed. They were both too busy and, without a word, he went back down the ladder and along the gangway to rejoin Daniel and Amy and Mrs Duggan.

But, as he did so, everything felt different. He found he was no longer worried or anxious, because he knew now that Mum and Dad were all right, that everything was all right.

It was a wonderful dream. It was just a pity that he had to wake up at the end of it.

CHAPTER ELEVEN

When William got up the next morning, he had made a decision. Brin had said that he could not manage the station on his own – and he was right – but William knew he didn't want anyone else to take over the job. He didn't want a stranger doing his father's work, sitting in his father's chair in the pantry, and using the tools in his workshop. When his parents came back from wherever they had been, William wanted them to find everything just as it had been when they left, so that life could carry on as before.

And there was only one way he could think of to make that happen.

Although it was still early, he got up, dressed and walked down the hill to Mrs Duggan's house.

He found her in the back garden, splitting logs with an axe, while Timber picked up the pieces and stacked them neatly in the shed. She stopped when she saw William.

'Any news?'

'Not really,' said William. 'Uncle Larry says it might be as long as a week before they know anything definite, and Brin says I can't manage the station that long on my own.'

'Ah.' Mrs Duggan leant thoughtfully on her axe. 'How they going to sort that out then?'

'I'm not sure,' said William, 'but I think I could manage, if you helped.'

'With the station?'

'Yes.'

'Not sure about that.' Mrs Duggan made a face. 'Looking after people . . . Not good with people. Never have been.'

'You wouldn't have to be,' said William. 'There's only two or three passengers a week and I can deal with them. What we need is someone who can help keep an eye on Daniel, help with the cooking, and maybe do the bricks once in a while. If you could do that, I could do all the people stuff.'

Mrs Duggan chewed thoughtfully at her bottom lip. 'Your Uncle Larry think of this?' she asked.

'No,' said William. 'It's my idea. I thought I'd ask you about it first.'

There was another pause.

'Might work,' said Mrs Duggan eventually.

'Could you come up to the house later?' asked William. 'And talk to Uncle Larry about it?'

Mrs Duggan considered this. 'Be up about eleven,' she said. 'All right?'

'That'd be great,' said William, and he was about to go when he remembered the other thing he had wanted to ask.

'You knew about the Portal,' he said, 'but you didn't say anything.'

'No,' Mrs Duggan admitted.

'So how did you know? I thought it was supposed to be a big secret.'

'It was,' said Mrs Duggan, 'but your dad . . .' She stopped. Whatever it was she had been going to say, she changed her mind. 'Long story. Maybe tell you one day.'

Down at the station, William waited until Emma told him that Uncle Larry was awake and then took in a tray with a pot of tea and a plate of chocolate biscuits. Dad had always said if you were going to ask someone to do something for you, you should make sure they were comfortable first.

'I thought you might like some tea,' he said, placing the tray on the table by the bed.

'Ah! How kind!' Uncle Larry pulled himself up to a sitting position.

'I was thinking about what Brin was saying, about my not being able to run the station on my own.' William began pouring out the tea. 'And I wondered if you'd thought of Mrs Duggan.'

'I have,' said Uncle Larry, 'but it wouldn't work. You couldn't ask Mrs Duggan to look after a passenger. She's not good with people.'

'She wouldn't have to be, would she?' William passed Uncle Larry the mug. 'I could do all that. What we need is someone to help with the house, keep an eye on Daniel, maybe do the bricks occasionally . . . and she could do that OK, couldn't she?'

Uncle Larry thought about it.

'It might work,' he said. 'I'll have a talk to her.'

'She's coming up to the farm at eleven,' said William. 'I'll tell you when she's here, shall I?'

'That would be . . . Yes. Thank you.'

'Right . . .' William turned to leave. 'And the bricks came ten minutes ago. You've got forty-three messages.'

Uncle Larry stared thoughtfully at the door for several seconds after William had gone. The boy was more like his father than he had realized, he thought. He had that same knack of coming up with the solution to a tricky problem, but making it sound as if he was asking your advice.

He smiled to himself and sipped his tea. He wasn't sure why but for some reason he was feeling much more cheerful.

The meeting at eleven o'clock lasted barely an hour. Uncle Larry, Brin, William and Mrs Duggan sat in the sitting room down in the station and Uncle Larry ran over what Mrs Duggan should do and how much she should be paid for doing it. Brin gave her a phone so that she could keep in touch with Emma even when she was out with the sheep, and William showed her how to use the lift down to the station by dialling 1066 on the office phone.

The only problem, as Mrs Duggan pointed out, was what they should do if a passenger arrived while William was at school, and it was William who suggested that he didn't go back to school at all.

'There's only three more days before the holidays,' he pointed out. 'How about someone rings in and says I'm still sick?'

'Sounds like the simplest solution,' Uncle Larry agreed. 'Let's do that then. Any other problems?'

'Amy won't mind, will she?' William looked at Mrs Duggan. 'Moving up here, I mean?'

'Can't see why,' said Mrs Duggan. 'Spends most of her time here anyway.'

'And Timber?' William looked across at the dog who had been following the conversation with rapt attention. 'He'll be happy sleeping in the kitchen or something, will he?'

'He's a dog,' said Mrs Duggan briefly. 'He'll do as he's told.'

Both Uncle Larry and Brin left that afternoon. Uncle Larry left first, after giving careful instructions on what William should do if Federation Security got in touch with news about his parents.

'You send me an emergency brick,' he said. 'Emma'll tell you how. And if a problem comes up you can't solve, tell Brin. He's closest and he can be straight over.' With a wave of his hand and a promise to be back in a week to see how things were going, he disappeared through the Portal.

Brin left an hour later after a ferocious burst of cleaning that left the station smelling rather heavily of bleach. 'You've got a passenger at four thirty,' he reminded William as he made his way to the Portal. 'You're sure you don't want me to stay and help?'

William said he thought he'd be OK.

'In that case I shall leave you to it . . .' Brin polished an invisible smudge of dirt from the wall, before stepping on to the Portal surface. 'Don't forget now. A message every day to tell me how it's going!'

Ten minutes after he'd gone, Mrs Duggan appeared outside the back door with six suitcases she had brought up on the tractor. Only one of them belonged to her. The other five were for Amy, and William helped carry them inside and up to Daniel's room. Mrs Duggan made up the beds and started unpacking, and then there was just time to get tea ready before Daniel and Amy got back from school.

At a quarter past four William went back down to the station to greet his next passenger.

Prince Helmut of Tarkis was a tall, good-looking young man, who was clearly a bit disappointed to find William in charge of the Portal.

'I don't mean to be rude,' he said, 'but I was really hoping to see your father.'

'I'm afraid he's away at the moment,' said William.

'Away? Do you know when he's going to be back?'

'Not really,' said William. 'Did you need him for anything urgent?'

'Well, it wasn't that important.' Prince Helmut spread himself out on a sofa in the station sitting room. 'I just wanted to tell him how well every-thing had worked out and . . . and say thank you.'

'Oh,' said William. 'Thank you for what?'

Prince Helmut's family, it turned out, had ruled the tiny world of Tarkis for more than three hundred years, but recently there had been demands for the King to abdicate.

'The people kept saying they wanted a parliament,' the Prince explained, 'and it looked like the end of the line for us royals. But then one day, on the way back from a holiday on Cygnus, your father tells my father that when the same thing happened here, your people chose to have a parliament and a monarchy. He told Dad exactly how they did it, Dad came home and tried it – and it worked! We're more popular now than we've ever been!'

'Oh, good,' said William.

'It is very good!' the Prince agreed. 'My father's having the time of his life, going around giving state banquets and military parades and so on, but . . .' His face clouded for a moment. 'I'm not quite sure what I'm supposed to do. While I'm waiting to be king. I was hoping your father might know.'

'We have a prince who's waiting to be king,' said William, 'but I'm not sure what he does.'

Prince Helmut looked up. 'Is there any way you could find out?'

William asked Emma to set up a connection with the Internet and then tapped Prince Charles into Google. There were quite a lot of sites about Prince Charles and Prince Helmut sat glued to the screen in the drawing room, furiously down-loading notes on to a recording device that hung round his neck. 'The Prince's Trust . . .' William heard him muttering, as he brought in tea and sandwiches. '. . . I want all the stuff on that. And the Duke of Edinburgh's Award. And I want lots of pictures of this garden at Highgrove . . .'

He was still at it nearly five hours later, when William brought him a last pot of tea and warned him it would soon be time to leave.

'Nearly finished!' said the Prince. 'There're some great ideas here! Can't imagine why I didn't think of them myself. I am very grateful to you!' He smiled happily at William. 'And I shall tell your father so next time I see him. Where is he, by the way?'

William admitted that he didn't know, and found himself telling Prince Helmut the story of his parents' disappearance.

'Extraordinary!' said the Prince when he'd finished. 'Has anyone thought of asking a Guardian?'

'I . . . I don't think so,' said William, who had no idea what a Guardian was.

'The Guardians have Touchstones,' said Prince Helmut. 'With a Touchstone you can find out anything that ever happened, anywhere.'

'Can you?' William wondered why Uncle Larry hadn't suggested this himself.

'Of course, everyone has lots of questions so there's a waiting list of ten or fifteen years,' said Prince Helmut, 'but one of the benefits of being in a royal family is that you get automatic access to a Guardian once a month.' He looked across at William. 'I could ask what's happened to your parents when I get home, if you were interested.'

'Oh, I am,' said William. 'Very interested. Thank you.'

When Prince Helmut had left, William came back upstairs and found Mrs Duggan clearing up in the kitchen.

'Children both asleep,' she said. 'Put out clean clothes for Daniel, and Timber's done the chickens.' The dog lay curled up in his basket by the cooker. His eyes opened briefly to look at William, then closed again. 'How did it go with His Majesty?'

'Not too bad,' said William.

Mrs Duggan wiped her hands on a towel and glanced round the kitchen to check there was nothing out of place. 'Thought I'd do the bricks tonight. Let you get a proper sleep.'

'OK,' said William. 'And I'll do getting up Daniel and Amy in the morning.'

'Right.' Mrs Duggan took a deep breath and looked out the window at the night sky for a moment. 'You reckon we can do this, do you?'

'I know we can,' said William. 'We can do it easy. You'll see.'

And, as he spoke, he tried very hard to sound as if he believed it.

Chapter Twelve

In one way, at least, it turned out to be easier than William had expected. Managing the Portal, he found, rather to his surprise, was really no problem at all. Doing the bricks and looking after the occasional passenger was comparatively simple now that Mrs Duggan was helping out.

The bit that wasn't quite so easy, was Daniel.

William was never sure how it started or why it went so badly wrong, but now that they were living in the same house, Daniel and Mrs Duggan didn't seem to get on at all. In fact, in a matter of days, things had got to the point where they could barely talk to each other without one of them losing their temper.

It puzzled William. Admittedly, it wasn't easy

living with someone who tended to leave parts of dead animals lying around, but that was just how Daniel was. Mrs Duggan, however, did not see it that way. When she found a half-eaten rabbit carcass on the breadboard, she would demand that Daniel throw it away. Daniel would say that he needed it for an experiment, Mrs Duggan would tell him not to argue, Daniel would argue . . . and in no time there'd be a full-blown row going on with all the sound effects of slamming doors and some very loud shouting.

William wondered if part of the problem was Daniel having to share a room with someone whose clothes took up all of the wardrobe and a good deal of the floor, and whose beauty-care products had taken over the desk. But Daniel said he didn't mind any of that. It was Mrs Duggan that was the problem and within a matter of days, the two of them could scarcely be in the same room together without one of them saying or doing something that made the other one explode.

William didn't know what to do. There had never been rows when his parents were here. He had seen arguments like this in his friends' houses, but never at home. Disagreements at home were sorted out before they ever got to be rows, though – now that he thought about it – he wasn't quite sure how this had happened.

After one particularly violent argument over a dead pigeon in the fridge, William tried asking Daniel not to argue with Mrs Duggan. 'She's helping look after us,' he said. 'Please, be nice to her!'

'Why should I?' said Daniel. 'She's always picking on me!'

William pointed out that he was the one who left dead pigeons in the fridge. 'If Mrs Duggan asks you to do something,' he said, 'you just have to do it.'

'No, I don't,' argued Daniel. 'She's not my mother.'

'But she's looking after us till Mum gets back,' said William. 'And we need her.'

'I don't,' said Daniel. 'And I'm not going to do what she says. She's ugly, and she smells.'

William was shocked. If Daniel had ever said anything like that in front of his father he would have . . . William thought for a moment. His father would obviously have done something to make sure it never happened again but . . . he wasn't sure what.

At the time, all William could think of to say was, 'That's very unfair. Mrs Duggan's working really hard and the least you can do is keep out of her hair until Mum and Dad get back from holiday.'

'When's that going to be?' said Daniel.

And of course William couldn't answer that.

He did his best to defuse the situation when he could. He tried to make sure he was around at the times Mrs Duggan and Daniel had to be together – like at meals or bedtime – to keep things calm. The evenings were particular danger points. Daniel would be tired and in need of careful handling, but Mrs Duggan didn't seem to know this. She would tell him not to do something, Daniel would do it, Mrs Duggan would shout at him, Daniel would shout back and off they'd go again.

As long as William was around, he could step in and steer one of them out of the room, but sometimes he wasn't there. Sometimes he was busy down at the station, looking after a passenger or the bricks, and it was on one such occasion that the Big Row happened.

William was looking after a passenger called Mrs Wharton, an elderly woman who wrote children's books and wanted to know what sort of stories William had enjoyed when he was smaller. He was telling her about The Very Hungry Caterpillar, when Amy rang down from upstairs and said simply, 'They're doing it again.'

It was nearly an hour before William could leave and go back upstairs, and by that time he found

Daniel in his bedroom – white, shaking with rage and silent. Somehow, the being silent was worse than if he'd been shouting and screaming.

'She's taken my skulls,' he said when William asked what had happened. He pointed to the empty shelves. 'All of them.'

'Why?' asked William.

It turned out this argument, like most, had begun with something very trivial. Mrs Duggan had told Daniel to pick up a sweet paper, Daniel said he wouldn't because he hadn't dropped it, Mrs Duggan told him to pick it up anyway, and finally things had escalated to the point where she told him that if he didn't she would take his skulls and throw them away. And she had.

William could hardly believe it. 'Why didn't you just pick it up?' he said.

'Why should I? I didn't drop it.'

'Does it matter?'

'Yes.'

William sighed.

'I can't stay here,' said Daniel. 'Not with her. I'm leaving home.'

'Don't be silly,' said William. 'Wait here. I'll go and talk to her.'

William found Mrs Duggan sitting on a log behind the barn, twisting and untwisting a length of barbed wire in her fingers, with Timber sitting beside her.

He had to tell her, William thought. He had to tell her that taking away Daniel's skulls for not picking up a sweet paper didn't make sense. He had to tell her she was supposed to be helping and that, at the moment, she wasn't. That with all the shouting and yelling, she was only making things worse.

He sat on the log beside her, trying to think how to say it, but it wasn't easy to tell someone old enough to be your mother that they were doing it all wrong and, without quite knowing why, he said nothing at all.

In the end, it was Mrs Duggan who spoke first.

'It was Timber,' she said.

'What?'

'That's how I knew about the Portal. It was Timber.' Mrs Duggan put the barbed wire carefully on the log beside her. 'Week I started work here, I ran over him with a tractor. Rope round his neck got caught in the axle, next thing, squeal, thump, and the back wheel's run over his head.'

'Oh,' said William, not quite sure where this conversation was going.

'Your dad heard the screams. Came running out with a medipac. I tell him it's no good, the dog's dead. He tells me to step back and then takes out this . . . this Life Support, and he picks up the dog and tells me to follow him inside.'

Mrs Duggan shook her head slowly as if she still found the whole thing hard to believe. 'Found out after what he'd done. Used his own life energy to keep Timber alive. Took him through the Portal. Got him patched up. Smarter than ever when they brought him back. Done something to his brain.'

She reached out a hand to scratch the top of Timber's head. 'Dog was all I had, then. Your dad knew that. Never forgotten it.' Mrs Duggan paused a moment before continuing. 'So when you ask me to help. Course I say yes. Chance to pay back, you see. Chance to say thank you.

'And I come up here and get it all wrong. Shouting and yelling. Make things worse instead of better. Wanted to help . . . Owed it to your dad . . . Wanted to help . . . Just get it all wrong . . .'

Mrs Duggan stared at the ground and a tear trickled down her cheek. It was big, like everything with Mrs Duggan, and it splashed on to the ground leaving a puddle the size of a saucer.

William had never heard her put so many words together in one speech – or in one week – and he reached out to put an arm round her. Mrs Duggan was too big for the arm to go all the way round, but he did it anyway.

'There has to be something we can do,' he said, 'to make things better.'

'Too late for that,' said Mrs Duggan gloomily. 'Daniel's never going to talk to me again.'

'I'm sure it's not too late,' said William, 'and you can leave Daniel to me. But I think we'll need to give him the skulls back.'

'Got them here.' Mrs Duggan pointed to a black plastic bag at her feet.

'Good.' William took the bag. 'He can have these when he's apologized, then you two can hug and make up.'

'Hug?' Mrs Duggan looked rather alarmed.

'It's all right,' said William. 'It was a figure of speech.'

Over the next few days, William spent some time explaining to Daniel how important it was to be patient with Mrs Duggan, and a lot of time talking to Mrs Duggan about the things that worked with Daniel and the things that didn't.

'Notice you never have a problem with him,' said Mrs Duggan gloomily as they stood in the kitchen after lunch one day, watching Daniel and Amy build a bear trap by the outhouse. 'You tell him to do something, he does it. I tell him and it's like I've asked him to throw himself out of a train.'

There was some truth to this but, thinking about it, William realized it was also true that he tried to avoid *telling* Daniel to do anything – unless it was something like not to use the chainsaw. Daniel was the sort of boy who, if you said he *had* to do something, would immediately want to do the opposite, and shouting at him would only make him want to even more. The trick with Daniel, if you really wanted him to do something, was to get him to agree to it in advance. Once he'd agreed to something, he didn't mind being told when it was time to get on and do it.

'And it helps, of course,' William added, 'if you've said nice things to him.'

'Nice things?' said Mrs Duggan. 'How do you mean?'

'Well,' said William, 'it's like what you do with Amy when you see her in a new outfit. You say "Oh, you look lovely, that really suits you!" That sort of thing.'

'Can't tell Daniel he looks lovely,' said Mrs Duggan. 'He doesn't.'

'No, you wouldn't say anything about him looking nice,' William agreed, 'but when he does something useful or helpful, you could say thank you and how grateful you were.'

'He doesn't *do* anything helpful,' said Mrs Duggan. 'He's no help at all, you know that!'

'He does things right occasionally,' said William. 'And when he does, if you say something nice, it means the next time you ask him to do something he'll be more likely to do it. That's how it works.'

'Is it?' said Mrs Duggan.

'Yes,' said William. 'I think it is.'

'All right,' said Mrs Duggan. 'I'll give it a try.'

And to be fair, she did. It took a considerable effort, but Mrs Duggan stopped shouting, she tried to find nice things to say to Daniel and she even gave him a hug occasionally, though to be honest neither of them seemed to get a lot of pleasure from it.

And things were better as a result. The house was quieter and calmer, and the rows mostly stopped, but William could not help but notice that Daniel was . . . different. The brother who could come rushing home with a dead hedgehog to cook, or to dissect the lungs from a mole, seemed to have gone. Instead, there was a Daniel who lay in bed a lot most of the day, watching endless hours of television. Sometimes, not even Amy could get him to move. He was, William suspected, deeply unhappy, but on the two occasions he asked what was wrong, Daniel only shrugged and turned away.

William knew what was wrong, of course. What

Daniel needed – what they all needed – was for his parents to come home and for everything to go back to the way it was supposed to be. But that wasn't going to happen, not for a while, anyway, and in the meantime William had no idea what he could do to help.

The man who did, oddly enough, was General Ghool.

CHAPTER THIRTEEN

General Ghool came breezing up through the Portal on his way to sort out a civil war on Parris. 'How's it going here?' he asked as William led him through to the sitting room. 'Heard anything about your parents yet?'

William told him that there was still no news. It was over two weeks now since the vet had found the bloodstained handbag in the quarry, but William was no nearer knowing the truth of what had happened to his mother and father. Federal Security had sent him two reports since then, but both said simply that no trace of his parents had been found and that the search was continuing.

'Very curious,' said the General. 'Are you following up any other lines of enquiry?'

'When Prince Helmut of Tarkis came through,' said William, 'he promised to ask a Guardian about it.'

'Now that's a smart move.' The General nodded approvingly. 'A Touchstone should give you the answer – and I hope the news is good.' He settled back in his chair and watched as William poured his tea. 'How's that brother of yours? Recovered from his blood poisoning, I hope?'

'He's fine,' said William. 'It's not his blood we're worried about at the moment.'

'Oh?' The General sipped his tea. 'What is it this time?'

William wasn't sure if it was polite to bother passengers with personal problems, but the General seemed genuinely interested and he found himself describing how Daniel seemed to have lost his enthusiasm for life, and how he spent most of his time lying in bed.

'Well, it's understandable,' said General Ghool. 'He's obviously very worried about his parents.'

'I know he misses them,' said William, 'but why should he be worried? He thinks they're on holiday in France.'

'You haven't told him the truth?'

'No,' said William. 'I thought that really would worry him.'

'Ah!' The General leant back in his chair. 'If

you'll forgive my saying so, I think that could be the problem.'

'Could it?'

'You can't hide something that big,' said the General. 'Your brother knows there's *something* wrong – he'll have picked up the signals – and if you're not telling him what it is, he'll know it must be something serious. Which must be very frightening for him. And being frightened usually comes out in bad behaviour and depression.'

'Oh . . .' William thought about this. 'So what should I do?'

'Tell him the truth,' said the General simply. 'First thing they teach you in the army is never to hide bad news from the troops. Good or bad, you always tell them the truth.'

'But I can't tell Daniel about the Portal . . . can I?'

'I don't see why not,' said the General. 'You'll need to ask Larry first, of course, and he might want you to use a mind-lock to make sure he doesn't accidentally tell anyone else but . . . tell him I thought it was important.'

'Right,' said William. 'I will.'

'And when you do tell Daniel, my advice is to keep it simple. Say your mum and dad have gone – you don't know where, but you're still trying to find them – and then ask for his help. Tell him you and Mrs Duggan can't manage everything on your own and you need him to help out with things.'

'What sort of things?' asked William.

'Stuff around the house . . .' The General waved his hands expansively. 'Anything at all, really, as long as it's proper work.'

'He's miserable enough already,' said William. 'If I tell him Mum and Dad have gone missing and then that he has to help round the house, he'll want to throw himself off a cliff.'

The General smiled. 'Funnily enough, that's not how it works. If you tell him the family's in trouble and needs his help, he'll *want* to do something – and he'll feel a lot better when he does.'

William was not entirely convinced by this, but said he would try it.

'And if it was me,' said the General, 'when I'd done that, I'd go one step further.'

'Yes?'

'I'd find something Daniel can do that he knows nobody else can. That's what'll really give him a boost.'

'He's only eight,' said William. 'I don't think there is anything like that.'

'Age has nothing to do with it,' said the General. 'We all have a special gift and in Daniel's case even I can see what it is.'

William thought about it. The only special gift

of Daniel's he could think of was his capacity to annoy Mrs Duggan to the point of despair.

'Daniel knows more about the wildlife around here than the rest of you put together, doesn't he?' General Ghool's eyes glinted under his shaggy eyebrows. 'Now . . . how could you put a skill like that to use?'

The next morning, William called a family meeting in the kitchen. Daniel and Amy sat on one side of the table, William and Mrs Duggan on the other, and William began by saying that he was going to tell them the truth about Mr and Mrs Seward. They stared at him, wide-eyed, as he told them about the Portal – Uncle Larry had agreed that Amy should be told as well as Daniel, as long as they had a mind-lock – and then took them down in the lift to see it for themselves.

Their eyes widened even more as he took them on a brief tour of the station before walking them through to the sitting room and explaining, as simply as he could, what had happened. He told them how Uncle Larry had gone searching up and down the Portal corridor, how he and Brin had searched the station, how Federal Security had searched the farm and the surrounding area and how, despite it all, nobody knew where Mr and Mrs Seward were.

'So where have they gone?' asked Daniel when he'd finished.

'We don't know,' said William.

'They could have been murdered,' suggested Amy.

'They could . . .' William did his best to sound calm and unworried. 'But Uncle Larry thinks if they'd been hurt in some way there'd be evidence of . . . something. The fact is we don't know what's happened to them, but we do know what we have to do while they're gone.' He looked across at their faces. 'We have to keep this place going. We have to keep the farm running, and the house, and the station, so that it's all still here when they get back. And it's going to take all of us to do that.'

'So far, Mrs Duggan and me have done all the jobs round the house, but it can't go on like that. Mrs Duggan's got enough to do running the farm, I'm busy with the station . . . so I've drawn up a list.' William produced a piece of paper. 'These are the jobs we need you to do.'

Amy and Daniel studied the list. There were a lot of things on it. Several chores for each day.

'Well?' said William.

'We have to do all this?' said Daniel.

'Yes,' said William. 'It's the only way it's going to work.'

'I don't want to do the hoovering,' said Daniel. 'I don't like hoovering.' He turned to Amy. 'If you do the hoovering, I'll do the washing-up and the chickens.'

'OK,' said Amy.

And that was when William thought they might be in with a chance.

You could feel the change almost at once. It was as if some pressure had been lifted. Something that had blocked the life flow of the family had been swept away and . . . well, it wasn't quite like the old days but it was certainly better than it had been.

What astonished William was how willingly his brother did everything on the list. Daniel had never done anything without complaining, but now he would bustle around as if his life depended on it. All the old resentment seemed to have disappeared overnight. He was back to laughing and joking and, best of all, Mrs Duggan wasn't the enemy any more. She was just prickly old Mrs Duggan and if she snapped at him, Daniel didn't snap back, but punched her on the arm and asked for something to eat.

And when William put the second part of the General's plan into effect, it got even better.

'The passengers sometimes like to go outside

for a walk,' he told Daniel one morning. 'It used to be Mum who took them, because she knew the names of all the plants and birds and things. I've got someone special coming today, and wondered if you'd do it.'

The special passenger who arrived that afternoon was Mrs Hepworth, the woman who had been rather offended when William had told her she was not allowed outside. She was on her way back to her home world near Deneb.

'I'm sorry about last time,' he said as he escorted her from the Portal to her room. 'I made a mistake. If you want to go outside at all today, my brother's all set to take you wherever you like.'

Mrs Hepworth was delighted. William had already put out some clothes for her and, as soon as she was changed, he took her upstairs. Daniel was waiting for them at the back door, with a pair of binoculars round his neck, several reference books in a pack on his back and a serious look on his face.

'I'm Daniel,' he said, holding out a hand, 'and I'm your guide for this afternoon. Is there anything in particular you wanted to see?'

'Well . . .' said Mrs Hepworth, 'if it's convenient, I'm particularly interested in birds. I've been told you have some species that not only fly but . . . go under water?'

'Yes, we do,' said Daniel. 'I can show you some of those.'

Mrs Hepworth beamed down at him. 'In that case, lead the way young man! Lead the way!'

Daniel led their visitor crawling through mud along the side of the river bank to show her a kingfisher. He made her wade through waist-deep water to look at a coot's nest, and then made her hide in a patch of nettles to see a heron spear a fish with its beak then carry it back to its young.

Mrs Hepworth came back to the farm nearly three hours later, covered in scratches, soaked to the skin, with mud all over her face and clothes, and a swelling on her right arm where she had been stung by a wasp.

And William had never seen anyone look so happy.

When Uncle Larry called in at the end of the week he said that Mrs Hepworth had been so impressed by the way she had been looked after that she had sent him a special message of thanks.

'So congratulations!' he said, as he sat with William on a couple of sun-loungers on the patio, looking out over the valley. 'And how are things going apart from the station? Is it any better between Daniel and Mrs Duggan yet?'

'They're fine now,' said William. 'It's been brilliant. They get on really well.'

'You're quite sure about that?' said Uncle Larry. 'I only ask, because they seem to be trying to kill each other at the moment.'

William looked over towards the barn, where Daniel and Amy were trying to force Mrs Duggan to the ground. Amy had flung herself round her mother's neck and Daniel had his arms wrapped tightly round her ankles.

'Do you think one of us should go over and stop them?'

'It's all right,' said William. 'They're only playing.'

The arms round the feet finally took effect and Mrs Duggan toppled like a great tree to the ground. With a whoop of triumph, Daniel and Amy sat on her back and began punching her.

'Playing?' said Uncle Larry doubtfully.

'Oh, yes!' William smiled. You couldn't help but admire the woman. The play fights were just what the children needed, and she was brilliant at it.

'Aren't they hurting her?' Uncle Larry winced as Amy jumped up and down on Mrs Duggan's stomach.

'They're just working off a bit of energy,' said William. 'It was another of General Ghool's ideas.'

'Ah!' Uncle Larry relaxed. 'Well, if he suggested it, I suppose it's all right. It's what he does for a living, after all.'

'Is it?'

'Oh, yes,' said Uncle Larry. 'You get a quarrel breaking out between two countries, and General Ghool's the man they send in to sort it out. One of the Federation's top troubleshooters. And I suppose sorting out a family's just the same thing on a smaller scale.'

He gazed out over the valley for a moment before continuing. 'I must say I'm impressed. Station running smoothly. Delighted passengers. Everything working the way it should.' He reached across and patted William's knee. 'All we need now is some good news about your parents, eh?'

CHAPTER FOURTEEN

Unfortunately, when the news came, it was not good. A message from Prince Helmut arrived a little before two o'clock the next morning, and William and Uncle Larry watched it together in the station kitchen.

'Greetings, William!' said the hologram of the Prince. 'Sorry not to have been in touch before, but you wouldn't believe how busy it's been! I've been working non-stop setting up this Trust thing – which has been *very* successful by the way. We've raised millions of credits and I've had thousands of letters of support, all very flattering! Anyway . . .' Prince Helmut paused briefly to gather his thoughts, '. . . you may remember I promised to ask the Guardian here what had happened to your parents and I have – but I'm afraid I didn't get much of an answer. The Guardian tells me his Touchstone has no idea what happened to your mother and father and . . . what?'

There was the murmur of another voice from somewhere to the Prince's side and he listened for a moment before turning back to William.

'He says his exact words are that he "cannot access the information you require", but he wants me to tell you there's no evidence of anyone, anywhere, wanting to do your parents harm. I don't know if that's any help but . . . well, it's all he has to say.' Prince Helmut looked briefly to his right to check this was the case before continuing. 'I hope you find out what happened to them at some point. I must go. Big charity dinner tonight! Good luck!'

'I thought,' William turned to Uncle Larry, 'that a Guardian with a Touchstone knew everything.'

'They do . . . mostly.' Uncle Larry frowned. 'But there is one limitation. They can only access an event from the Great Memory if that event has been held in the mind of at least two conscious entities. Otherwise it's too small to retrieve.'

William wasn't quite sure what this meant.

'It means,' said Uncle Larry, 'that whatever happened to your mother and father, there are no two people who know what it was.' He began pacing up and down, his forehead wrinkled in a deep frown. 'Which I suppose is helpful in a way.'

'Is it?'

'Well, it means we can rule out certain things.' Uncle Larry ticked the items off on his fingers. 'We know now that your parents didn't go off anywhere together. We know they can't have been kidnapped and we also know that whatever happened to one of them must have happened without the other one knowing. Because any of those things would involve two people knowing about what happened, and if two people knew, the Guardian would have been able to tell us about it. On the same logic, we also know that no one has seen your parents or spoken to them since the day they disappeared.'

'But that's not possible, is it?' asked William.

'No,' said Uncle Larry, 'it's not.' He paused. 'Except that it seems to be what's happened.'

The news was rather discouraging, and William wondered whether he should tell the others, until he remembered what the General had said about not hiding bad news from the troops. He told them at breakfast, explaining as well as he could what Uncle Larry had said about the Guardians and Touchstones, and was surprised how well they took it.

'Have to manage on our own a bit longer then,' said Mrs Duggan when he'd finished, 'but I reckon we can do that. Done it before, do it again.' She looked down at Daniel and Amy sitting either side of her and the children nodded their agreement. 'So let's get on with it, eh?'

Amy set about clearing up breakfast, Daniel went outside to do the chickens and Timber started loading washing from the basket into the machine. It was only later that morning that Daniel expressed any visible anxiety. He came into the office, where William was working out Mrs Duggan's money, and asked, 'You don't think they're dead, do you?'

'No, I don't,' said William. 'I don't know why, but . . . I don't.'

'No. Me neither.' Daniel stared out of the window for a moment and then asked if he and Amy could dig out a swimming pool behind the barn.

'Only with shovels and spades,' William told him. 'No jack hammers and no digging under buildings. Remember what happened to the outhouse wall.'

For the next week, things went fairly smoothly. The bricks came and went. There were three passengers through the Portal – none of whom caused any difficulties – and when Brin arrived on Saturday to check how things were going he said he couldn't have run the place better himself. In fact, things were going so smoothly that William had time to take up a new hobby.

It started with a passenger called Porlock who, like Hippo White, had left something for William's father to repair and asked, soon after he arrived, if it was ready to collect yet.

'I don't want to be a nuisance,' he said, 'but I was hoping to give it to my son for his birthday.'

William said he didn't know if the repairs had been completed, but offered to take Porlock down to the workshop and check. They found the object – it was a small, brightly coloured cube – but according to the workbook, although William's father had found the fault – a burnt-out circuit board – and even made a replacement, it had not yet been fitted.

William picked up the cube, and asked what it was.

'It's a toy,' said Porlock. 'It makes this *zzzip* when it moves and *bop* when it stops. and then *whirrrrrs* when it stands still. My father gave it to me when I was little and . . . and I was very fond of it.'

He looked, William saw, extremely disappointed and later that morning, while Porlock was out with Daniel, it occurred to William to ask Emma if fitting the new circuit board would be a complicated or difficult business. The station computer told him that it wasn't.

'Do you think I could do it?' William asked. 'I mean, I don't want to damage it or anything.'

'The task is not complicated,' said Emma. 'I estimate you could complete it in ten minutes.'

With Emma telling him what to do, the repair actually took less than five. It was a simple matter of removing the outer casing – held in place by magnets rather than screws – sliding the new circuit board into position and then putting the whole thing together. He gave the finished item to Porlock when he returned from his walk and his face lit up with delight.

'I think it's all right,' William told him, 'but I haven't tried it out yet.'

'Well, let's do that now, shall we?' Porlock took the toy, twisted the lid, pressed each of the two green buttons on the bottom and placed it back on the floor. With a *zzzzip* sound it began to move, marching across the carpet, and then disappeared.

William was wondering where it had gone, when he heard a *brrrr* noise and spun round to find the toy chugging up from behind. For some reason the sight of it made him laugh.

'Believe me,' said Porlock, 'if you're two years old, you can't get enough of it! It's such a marvellous little toy!' His face beamed with pleasure. 'And I'm very grateful!'

'Well, it wasn't really me,' said William. 'Dad had done the tricky bit.'

'Of course.' Porlock was still staring at the toy, moving around the floor. 'I hope you'll let him know how much I appreciate it? When he gets back?'

'Yes,' said William. 'Yes, I will.'

After that, William started spending quite a lot of his time down at the workshop. In the hours when he had to be on call for a passenger, or in the evenings, when Timber was looking after Daniel and Amy, the workshop was where he could usually be found.

At first, he simply looked at things, and asked Emma to explain what they were. Amongst the items on the table, laid out for repair, he found a suitcase that made whatever you put in it weigh less, a machine that taught you maths by stimulating the pleasure centres in your brain when you got the right answer, and a buzzbot with a built-in shield, that could follow someone and send back pictures of whatever they were doing.

Almost as interesting as any of the objects he found were the tools William's father used to repair them. There were devices that could see inside machines so that you didn't have to take them apart to find out what was wrong. There were saws that worked without noise or effort and that could cut with an accuracy measured in nanometres, and glues and welders that could join anything to anything with a bond that was both unbreakable and invisible.

In the shelves and cabinets on the walls on each side of the workshop were boxes and drawers containing thousands of components and parts that could be used to build or repair almost anything. William wondered where his father had acquired them all and it was Brin who told him they had mostly come from passengers. All the regulars knew of his father's passion for old machines and they would bring him odd items they knew might interest him.

From looking at the tools and finding out what they did, it was a short step for William to start using them. According to Emma, there were several items on his father's list which, like Porlock's marvellous little toy, were fairly simple to repair. He worked cautiously, only tackling jobs that the station computer thought were suitable and, in the course of the next two weeks, restored a working model of a Star Portal (including figures that would vanish and reappear) and a device called a Universal Coat, which apparently kept you warm and dry in even the coldest and wettest weather.

The weather outside was in fact deliciously warm and sunny, but William found himself spending more and more time in the lower level of the station, and it was while he was down there that he found half a dozen shields in one of the drawers at the back of his father's workshop. He gave them to Daniel.

'I thought if you had these when you took passengers out for a walk,' he said, passing Daniel the egg-shaped objects after explaining what they did, 'you could get right up close to animals and things, and they'd never know you were there.'

He was nearly right. As Daniel pointed out, you still had to be careful about being upwind and not making any noise, but if his tours of the surrounding fields and woodland had been impressive before, the results when he and his party were invisible were truly extraordinary. Passengers came back having seen the most astonishing sights, and whenever any of them wrote afterwards to say thank you for their stay, Daniel's 'tours' were almost always top of the list of things they had enjoyed.

Though not all Daniel's 'trips' went as smoothly as he would have liked.

CHAPTER FIFTEEN

Aventa and her two cousins arrived on a Tuesday evening and William knew they were going to be trouble even before the first of them floated up through the Portal. Brin had sent him a warning with the bricks two hours before.

'Watch out for these three,' his message had said. 'Lock up the alcohol, and *don't* let them out of the station.'

Not quite sure what to expect, William had cleared the drinks cupboard in the sitting room, told Emma not to let anyone up to the house unaccompanied, and locked the doors to all the rooms in the station that weren't for public access.

The girls were slightly older than William and, as they floated up in turn through the Portal, the first thing he noticed was that they were all alarmingly beautiful. Derma was short, with dark curly hair and soft, full lips, Hermione was taller with long, straight hair that hung down her back, and Aventa, the last to arrive, had the biggest, brownest, shiniest eyes that William had ever seen.

As he tried to say a few words of welcome, the girls were already moving past him and out to the lobby. Derma walked straight across to the sitting room, saying she was thirsty. Hermione, after trying the handles on several doors, disappeared into the wardrobe room and William found himself standing in the lobby with Aventa.

'What's your name?' she asked, standing rather closer to William than was comfortable.

'William,' he said, 'and if there's anything you'd like me to –'

'What we'd like, William . . .' Aventa moved even closer, '. . . is a little trip outside. Do you think you could arrange that?'

'I'm sorry.' William blushed. 'But this is a restricted planet . . .'

'We know it's restricted.' Derma had appeared from the clothes room with half a dozen dresses over one arm. 'That's why we want to go outside.'

'All those things that nobody's allowed to see!' Hermione emerged from the drawing room with a glass in one hand and a miniature bottle of apricot brandy that William had somehow missed. 'That's what makes it so exciting!'

'We know you're not supposed to let people out,' said Aventa, 'but you do, don't you?'

All three girls were standing very close to William. Hermione had taken his arm on one side and Derma was resting her head on his shoulder on the other.

'We just want to see what it's like, you know?' Aventa's voice was low and husky. 'It wouldn't be for long and we'd promise to do whatever you said.'

William found himself sweating slightly. 'I'm sorry.' He tried to keep his voice low and calm. 'But . . . it's not possible.'

'No?' Aventa moved even closer and looked up at William with large, appealing eyes. 'Are you sure? Not even for a few minutes?'

William hesitated, but only for a moment. He had come across girls like Aventa before. In his tutor group at school there had been a girl called Zara, who had been able to persuade boys to do almost anything. Even male members of staff had been known to melt under her gaze and calmly agree that, yes, it would be fine if her coursework was handed in a month late. He knew that if he once let these girls outside, he would be lost.

'I'm sorry,' he repeated firmly, 'but no.'

'Ah, well . . .' Aventa smiled, and tapped gently with her forefinger on her lower lip. 'If we can't go outside, we'll have to think of something else to do, won't we?' The eyes grew even bigger and rounder. 'Do you have any suggestions . . . William?'

William showed the girls the kitchen. There were, he explained, several items of Earth food that were usually popular with visitors and, if they wished, he would be happy to provide them. It was with a certain amount of relief – and a tinge of disappointment – that he watched them go off to their rooms, and he was left alone with the cooking.

His cooking was rather good these days, and he was busy for almost an hour, making a ham and mushroom pizza and a chocolate cake before coming back out to the lobby, where the first thing that struck him was the quiet.

'Where are they?' he asked Emma. 'Is everything all right?'

'The passengers,' Emma told him, 'have left the station and –'

'What?' A wave of panic went through William's body. 'What do you mean they've left? How did they get out without the password?'

'Your brother came down to see if they would like to take a trip outside,' said Emma, 'and the girls accepted. I think you'll find . . .'

William was not listening. He was already striding to the lift and, once upstairs in the house, calling for his brother. It was no good. Walking through to the kitchen, he knew the house was empty. The girls had gone.

As William stood outside the back door of the farmhouse, kicking himself for not keeping a closer eye on them and wondering what to do next, Daniel and Amy appeared, running up the path from the valley.

'What happened?' demanded William. 'Where are they?'

'They've gone,' said Daniel, his face white and scared. 'I took them down to the river and they . . . disappeared.'

The story came out in bits and pieces, with Amy chipping in the odd detail. Daniel had come down to the station to ask William if his passengers might be interested in a trip outside and Aventa had met him in the central lobby. She had told him they were definitely interested and that William had told them all about his brother and the amazing trips that he organized, and the sooner they started the better.

'She told us you didn't want to be disturbed as you were busy in the kitchen,' said Amy, 'so Daniel took them upstairs.'

'Down by the river, I gave them the shields,'

said Daniel miserably, 'so we could get close to a swan's nest and they . . . disappeared.'

'You don't think the same thing's happened to them as to your parents, do you?' asked Amy.

'No,' said William. 'This is quite different. Call your mother, will you? We may need Timber to help track them down.'

In fact, William found the girls without Timber. On a still summer's evening sound travels for miles, and the noise of three giggling, whooping girls gave William a fair indication of where they were.

They were on the road past the junction at the bottom of the hill, playing a game with passing cars. When William arrived he was in time to see Aventa, in a long white dress, standing in the middle of the road, waving her hands to stop a large, silver Mercedes. As the car slowed to a stop and the elderly woman inside wound down her window to ask if she could help, Aventa's answer was to stare at her for a moment, then disappear. At the same time, the other girls, also holding shields that made them invisible, opened and closed the side doors on the car, while Aventa suddenly reappeared with her face only inches from the terrified driver who screamed, slammed the car into gear and drove off as fast as she could, leaving the three girls doubled up with laughter in the road.

'All right,' said William. 'We're going back to the station now.'

The girls spun round to face him.

'We will come back when we're ready,' said Hermione haughtily.

'No,' said William. 'You have to come back now.'

'He doesn't seem to understand, does he,' said Derma, 'that we tell him what to do, not the other way round?'

'Ignore him,' said Aventa. 'Come on!' And she blinked out of view. An instant later the other girls did the same.

William turned on the torch that he had been given by Hippo White and the figures of the three girls showed up as green-glowing silhouettes, standing in the middle of the road.

'You've got thirty seconds,' he said. 'If you don't turn round and start walking back to the station in that time I'm going to use this.'

There was a moment's silence as the three girls looked at the torch William was holding in one hand, and the gun he carried in the other. Derma took a step towards the woods on her right.

'If you try and run off into the trees,' said William, 'you don't even get the thirty seconds.'

Derma stopped moving.

'How dare you! How *dare* you point that thing at me!' Aventa's huge eyes were filled with anger. 'Do you know who I am? Do you know who my father is?'

'Twenty seconds,' said William. 'And I really would advise you to start walking.'

'We are not walking anywhere!' said Aventa proudly. 'My father is the fourth richest man in the Federation, and when he hears that someone threatened me with a gun, you will wish you had never been born. We will come back to the station when we want to and when we do you had better be ready with an apology.'

'Ten seconds,' said William.

'You're bluffing,' said Aventa. 'You'd never dare!'

As the last seconds ticked away, William could see the dawning realization in Aventa's eyes that she might have made a mistake. But none of them were moving back to the farmhouse by then, so he shot them.

The PS11, commonly known as a wham-gun, acts directly on the motor signals from the brain, cutting off all orders that might move any of the body's major muscle groups. Rather cleverly, organs, like the heart, lungs and even the eyelids are not affected, so that anyone shot by a PS11 is still able to see, think and breathe. They just can't do anything else.

William was pulling the last of the three bodies to the side of the road when Timber appeared, followed by Mrs Duggan on a tractor.

'Need any help?' she said as she turned off the engine and climbed down.

'I could do with a hand getting them back to the house,' said William.

'No problem.' Mrs Duggan bent down to lift the body of Derma and slung it briskly over her shoulder. 'Plenty of room on the floor of the cab.'

William let Mrs Duggan carry the three girls down to the station, where she draped them over the bed and sofa in the blue suite. Then he locked the door and left them there for the hour or so it would take for the effects of the wham-gun to wear off.

When he came back, all three girls were beginning to move.

'You'll have to stay in here,' William told them, 'until it's time to leave. If you try and get out before that time, I've told the station computer to disable you.'

'You are *so* going to regret this,' said Aventa.

'Possibly.' William pushed a trolley into the room and placed it by the wall. 'This is food and something to drink if you're interested. I'll be back when it's time to take you to the Portal.'

'When my father hears about this . . .' hissed Aventa.

'I should imagine he already has,' said William. 'I've sent him an official complaint about you with recordings of everything that happened in the station and what you were doing to the old lady in the car.'

Aventa looked rather pale and, for the first time, all three girls seemed at a loss for words.

'I believe it's quite a serious offence,' William went on, 'deceitfully obtaining illegal access to a restricted planet – and that the penalties can be quite severe. I've also asked that none of you be allowed to travel through this Portal again without the presence of a responsible adult.' He looked at his watch. 'I'll be back in about two hours.'

For the next two hours, William sat in his father's pantry on the opposite side of the lobby where he could keep an eye on the door to the blue suite. He didn't think the girls could get out, but he kept the PS11 on the desk in front of him in case.

He had half expected the girls to make a fuss and steeled himself for a period of demented screaming, shouting and demands for their release but, to his surprise, there was not a sound from inside their room. For two hours he sat in the pantry, waiting, and then, as the last minutes ticked slowly away, he went back to the blue suite and knocked on the door.

Inside, he found Derma and Hermione lying on the bed and Aventa sitting on the floor painting her toenails.

'If you'd pack your things and get ready to leave,' he announced. 'The Portal will be ready in five minutes.'

Derma and Hermione stood up and stalked off to the bathroom and William was turning to leave when Aventa asked, 'Did you really send a message of complaint to my father?'

'Yes,' said William, 'though I don't suppose he'll take much notice of it.'

'Oh, yes, he will!' said Aventa. 'He threatened to send me to a reformatory if anything like this happened again, and he might just be angry enough to do it this time.'

'I think,' said William slowly, 'that you'll probably talk him out of it. It's what you're good at, isn't it? Making people do what you want.'

'Yes . . .' Aventa finished the nails on one foot and turned to the other. 'But it's not going to be easy this time, it really isn't.' She looked up and, to William's surprise, smiled. It wasn't one of her dazzling you-will-do-what-I-want-won't-you smiles but a rather shy, straightforward grin. 'Honestly! Why did you have to make such a big deal about a little trip outside? We weren't going to hurt anyone!'

'No?' William looked at her. 'My brother was terrified. Doing that to an eight-year-old's OK, is it?'

Aventa blushed.

'And the old woman in the car? Frightening her to death and then sending her off down the road, screaming her head off? That was OK too, was it?'

'It was just a bit of fun!'

'Yes, of course,' said William. 'I remember looking at her face and thinking how much she was enjoying herself.'

Aventa put down the nail polish. 'You really don't like me, do you?'

'As a matter of fact,' said William, 'I like you a lot. I just wouldn't trust you an inch, that's all.' He paused. 'I should have been more careful. You'd never have got out if Dad had been here.'

'I met him once,' said Aventa.

'My dad?'

Aventa nodded. 'I came through here when I was little. My nurse was taking me to Ferris, and I was making a bit of a fuss because I didn't want to leave home, and your dad . . . I don't remember what he said to me exactly, but he sat and talked to me and I remember, somehow, he made me think everything was going to be OK.'

'Yes,' said William, 'he was good at that.'

'What happened to him? Has he left or something?'

William was about to reply, when Emma's voice chimed in from the ceiling to say that it was nearly half past twelve.

'It's a long story,' said William. 'Time to go.' He stood up and knocked on the door to the bathroom.

'We'll be out in a minute,' said Derma.

'You've got thirty seconds,' said William, 'or I'm coming in to get you.'

There were the sounds of hurried movement from inside the bathroom, and Derma and Hermione scuttled out. William led the three girls across the lobby to the Portal and then watched them leave, as they had arrived, one by one.

Aventa was the last to go.

'Could you tell your brother . . .' she said, as she stepped on to the surface of the Portal, '. . . that I'm sorry if I frightened him? And I wish . . .' she looked directly at William. 'I wish . . .'

But she never got to say what she wished, because at that moment the Portal opened up beneath her feet, and she was gone.

CHAPTER SIXTEEN

When Uncle Larry arrived early the next day, he said that shooting passengers was not something the service normally encouraged, but admitted that, in the circumstances, he didn't know what else William could have done. Letting the girls roam loose in the countryside could have been disastrous.

'It's just unfortunate,' he added, 'that you were dealing with the daughter of one of the most powerful people in the Federation. When you upset someone like Silas T. Barnes, he can find ways to make life very uncomfortable for you, however right you may have been.'

'And you think I've upset him?'

'I'd say shooting his daughter might mean you're not on his Christmas list,' said Uncle Larry, 'but if he does make a fuss we can point out that you could have made it much worse. You could have reported the girls to Federation Security – in which case they'd still be locked up – and you could have sold the whole story to the news networks. So in a way he ought to be grateful.' Uncle Larry sipped thoughtfully at his tea. 'Let's hope Silas sees it that way, eh?'

A message from Silas T. Barnes arrived the following morning and, to William's relief and Uncle Larry's surprise, it contained neither complaints nor threats of revenge.

The hologram was of a small, ordinary-looking man with large brown eyes, standing in what looked like the main waiting area of a railway terminus, except that all the trains were floating several feet above the ground.

'I got your message, Mr Seward,' said the hologram briskly, 'and I would like to offer my sincere apologies for the behaviour of my daughter and her cousins while they were on your station. My daughter has told me it was entirely her fault and I hope you will accept the attached credit note as a small compensation for the trouble you were caused.'

It looked for a moment as if he was going to say something else, but there was someone talking to him and Mr Barnes gave a brief nod and the hologram abruptly switched off.

'His daughter told him it was her fault?' said Uncle Larry. 'Well, I'm jiggered! I thought she'd be the one screaming for revenge. And Emma tells me the small compensation is a hundred credits!' Uncle Larry patted William on the shoulder. 'That should buy you a few star-miles. But promise me you won't shoot any more passengers for a month or two, eh?'

Fortunately, in the weeks that followed, William didn't have to shoot anybody. Some of the passengers were a little more demanding than others but he was learning how to handle even these.

It was not the way he had expected to spend his summer holidays and part of him, particularly at the start, had missed being with friends. He had felt a pang when Craig rang up to ask if he could come over, or David's mother called to ask if he'd like to go swimming but, as time went by, the regrets had lessened. After all, it wasn't everyone who had a chance to look after a Star Portal. It was interesting, and so were the people who came through it. William liked meeting them, he liked being with them . . . and there was something else.

Rather to his surprise, he had noticed that, important and wealthy though the passengers might be – and most of them were – when they

came through the Portal they all needed something. Some just wanted peace and quiet, others
wanted entertaining, some needed exercise . . .
But it was very satisfying somehow to be the one
who could provide it and send them off six hours
later, happy and relaxed.

Like the time Mr Forrester, the manager of one
of the Federation's largest banks came up through
the Portal. He was a tall, worried-looking man
with steel-grey hair, a tightly buttoned black jacket
and an almost permanent frown. When William
welcomed him to the station, his reply was no
more than a curt nod as he walked straight through
to the sitting room, saying that he had a great
deal of work to do and would appreciate it if he
was not disturbed *at all* for the duration of his
stay.

It left William with a difficult choice because
the week before, down in his father's workshop,
he had found what Emma told him was a model
of a Wrovian battlecruiser, with a note attached
in his father's handwriting that said simply *Gift –
for Mr Forrester*. It was a wonderfully detailed
model, but the bank manager didn't look like the
sort of person who'd want to be given a toy space-
ship, especially after he'd asked not to be disturbed
under any circumstances.

Should William go in and give him the model

anyway? Should he wait until Mr Forrester was about to leave and give it to him then? Or would it be better to leave the whole thing until the next time he came through, when perhaps he wasn't so busy?

William was still thinking about it when, two hours later, Emma said that Mr Forrester had requested a glass of water. He got a jug and a glass from the kitchen and, as an afterthought, placed the model on the tray beside them. In the sitting room, Mr Forrester was sitting on the sofa, studying a hologram that seemed to consist of nothing but numbers. William put the tray on the table and was about to leave when he was called back.

'What's this?' Mr Forrester asked, pointing to the model.

'It's from my father,' William explained. 'I think it's a Wrovian battlecruiser.'

'You're nearly right . . .' Mr Forrester picked up the model and studied it. 'It is in fact a Y Class Fleet Command battlecruiser whose name translates as the *Don't Mess With Me*. She took part in the Borgan Wars and was lost with all hands in the Battle of Gravelans.' He looked at William. 'Your father wanted me to have this?'

'Yes,' said William. 'There was a note on it reminding him to give it to you next time you came through.'

'And how much do I owe him?'

'Oh, nothing,' said William. 'It's a gift.'

'Well, that certainly sounds like your father.' For the first time a faint smile flickered across Mr Forrester's lips. 'I remember, when I told him how we could make a fortune by re-opening the Old Star Portals, all he said was that money wasn't everything!'

William wondered why anyone would want to use the Old Portals. 'Didn't they take three and a half years just to get to Q'Vaar?' he asked.

'They did,' said Mr Forrester, 'and, as I explained to your father, that is exactly the point. You go to Q'Vaar at the speed of light, you come straight back again, and to you it's taken no time at all but your bank account has been sitting there gathering interest for seven years. A lot of people would pay good money for that to happen!'

He leant forward, clicked off the hologram with the numbers and then gestured to the *Don't Mess With Me*. 'Would it be possible to take this outside?'

The *Don't Mess With Me* was a working model. It was controlled by a cylinder the size of a tube of Smarties, and Mr Forrester was surprisingly good at it. Standing on the lawn at the back of the house, William watched as white flames appeared from the engine pods and the ship lifted slowly from the ground, banked to the right, and began picking up speed. Within seconds it was circling the garden faster than William would have thought possible, weaving in and out between the barn and the chicken run, spinning and rolling, changing direction, standing on its end, and finally coming to a halt a metre or two in front of William's astonished gaze.

'Wow!' he said.

'There's more!' Mr Forrester told him. 'She's a warship, so she's fitted with Starbolt cannon and Blackhead torpedoes. I'll show you what an attack run looks like . . .'

The ship moved up and off to the right until it was barely visible in the sky, and then came screaming back towards William. As it did so, a beam of light shot out from the front, then another from the back, and a moment later it was firing bolts of light from all sides and all angles, some a dazzling white, some huge, lazy pulses of green that floated towards the ground and then exploded in a shower of sparks. It was like watching a miniature fireworks display, and the noise that accompanied it all was equally dramatic, though Mr Forrester assured him there was no risk of damage.

'It's all just light and noise,' he said. 'Can't do any harm.' He held out the controls to Daniel, who had appeared with Amy from the back of the barn to see what was going on. 'You want to try it?'

William was not sure this was wise – his brother would almost certainly run the ship into a wall and break it – but Mr Forrester insisted it was perfectly safe.

'These things are virtually indestructible,' he said. 'At least while the force-field's turned on.' He thrust the controls into Daniel's hands. 'Go on, give it a whirl!'

The controls took a little mastering – it was all a matter of where you pointed the tube and how hard you gripped it with which fingers – but Daniel had the machine running in the end and even did a bombing run that launched two torpedoes neatly through the bathroom window.

'I've been collecting Starfleet warships for nearly twenty years now,' said Mr Forrester to William as they watched. 'I knew your dad came across these things sometimes so I asked him to keep an eye out for me. I never thought he'd find something this good, though!'

Mrs Duggan came out then with some tea, and they all sat round the big slatted table on the terrace for scones with cream and jam. As they ate, Mr Forrester told them how, on his home world, collectors would meet and re-enact some of the great battles of the Years of Chaos, with whole fleets of model ships racing around the sky firing at each other. Then Amy told him that Daniel had a collection of skulls and Mr Forrester said he would like to see it, so Daniel brought some of them down to show him.

William had to go and do the bricks at that point and, when he came back, he found Mr Forrester alone on the terrace. He had taken off his jacket and was sitting in his shirtsleeves in the late afternoon sun, quietly whistling to himself, while the *Don't Mess With Me* floated gently in the air in front of him.

'Mrs Duggan had to go and do something to a sheep,' he said when he saw William, 'and your brother and his friend have gone down to the river. They said we could join them if we wanted.'

'I'm sorry,' said William, 'but it's time to go now.'

'Goodness, already? Right.' Mr Forrester picked up his jacket and then turned off the *Don't Mess With Me*. 'I've promised to bring your brother the skull of a bilkrat, next time I come through,' he said. 'They have five interlocking jaws. I think he'd like it.'

'That's very kind of you,' said William. 'I'm sure he would.'

'And of course you'll thank your father for this,' Mr Forrester said, tucking the *Don't Mess With*

Me carefully under one arm, 'when he gets back from wherever it is he's gone?'

'Yes, of course,' said William.

Down in the station, before stepping on to the Portal, Mr Forrester turned and shook hands. 'Well, thank you again. For everything. It's been a very pleasant stopover. Really very pleasant indeed!'

'It was a pleasure,' said William, and the curious thing was that he meant it. For reasons he didn't entirely understand there was something very rewarding about watching someone like Mr Forrester arrive, tense and irritable, and seeing him leave, as he did now, relaxed and smiling.

It gave him the sort of buzz that Daniel might get from finding the skull of a kestrel, or Amy from trying on a designer dress. For some reason, it felt . . . *right*.

What didn't feel right was the way the weeks continued to pass without any news of his parents. The Federation Security Forces still delivered reports saying they had investigated this avenue or that, and Uncle Larry would explain when he visited that he was having someone analyse the contents of Mr Seward's personal files in Emma, or that they were trying to find a match with any similar disappearances on other worlds . . . but none of it ever seemed to lead anywhere.

His parents had disappeared, literally without a trace. Not only did nobody know what had happened to them, no one had any idea what *might* have happened or where they could look. It was only a week or so now until the end of the summer holidays and there had been discussions about what they might do if there was still no news by the time William had to go back to school.

The prospect alarmed William, not because he didn't like school, but because he still could not believe that so many weeks could have gone by without anyone being even a step closer to solving the mystery.

And, afterwards, he sometimes wondered if it might not have gone on like that forever, if it hadn't been for Lady Dubb.

CHAPTER SEVENTEEN

Lady Dubb's first claim to fame was that she had survived the wreck of the *Corinthian*. The huge passenger liner, pride of the Vangarian fleet, had disappeared on its maiden voyage somewhere in the Crab Nebula, and the only trace of her existence that had ever been found was the three-year-old Lady Dubb in a life pod.

Since that day, she had regarded it as her duty to live as full a life as possible and she had certainly fulfilled her promise. Lady Dubb had made and lost several fortunes, married and divorced three Federation Presidents and given birth to thirty-seven children. She was, as they say, a bit of a character and even William, who barely glanced at the Federation news, had heard of her.

She was a short, dumpy woman, but filled with an unstoppable energy. William reckoned that if you put a couple of jump leads on her fingers Lady Dubb could start a bus, and she was certainly not one of the passengers who left you wondering what it was they really wanted. If Lady Dubb wanted something, she told you, in the sort of voice that left you in no doubt that you were expected to go and get it.

'You're not Jack,' she said as she stepped out of the Portal. 'Where's Mr Seward?'

'My father's not here,' said William, 'but if there's anything you want –'

'What I want, young man,' said Lady Dubb, 'is a game of Monopoly. Your father promised me one the next time I came through. Where is he?'

William explained that his parents were away, but that a game of Monopoly would not be a problem. He would get the board and set it up in the sitting room.

'I'm going to be the battleship,' said Lady Dubb, 'and I'll tell you now you're not going to win as easily as your father did.' She followed William into the sitting room. 'And let's have some music. Last time I was here we had something by . . . what was his name . . . began with a W . . .'

'Mozart,' said William, who had checked with

Emma on what Lady Dubb had enjoyed in previous visits.

'That's the fellow!' She settled herself on the sofa with a smile. 'Let's have some of him.'

The game took a long time to play, partly because Lady Dubb took a break in the middle to go for a walk with Daniel, but mostly because, from the moment she arrived, Lady Dubb talked more or less continually. She talked about where she was going and why, about things that had happened to her in the past and that she hoped would happen in the future – and she asked a lot of questions.

'There's a story going round that you shot Aventa Barnes and her cousins,' she said. 'Is it true?'

William, blushing slightly, admitted that it was, and then had to describe what had happened.

'You got an apology out of Silas, did you?' said Lady Dubb with a chuckle when he'd finished. 'That's quite an achievement. But he was lucky you didn't hand her straight over to Security. When I see him, I'll tell him he got off lightly.'

'You know him?'

'Oh, everybody knows Silas!' Lady Dubb threw the dice and landed in jail again. 'Lovely man. Useless father, though. What Aventa needed was someone like your dad to sort her out. Where is he, by the way?'

William found himself telling her the whole story. He described the day he had come home and found the house empty, how Uncle Larry had arrived and searched everywhere and then how all the efforts to find out where his parents had gone had failed. As a result, four hours after she had arrived, they were still only halfway through the game when Lady Dubb leant back in her chair and asked for something to eat.

'I'm feeling a bit light-headed,' she said. 'Do you think you could make me a sandwich? And something to drink,' she added as William went off to the kitchen.

William made a toasted cheese sandwich and put it on a tray with a bottle of beer – according to Emma they were Lady Dubb's favourites – and carried them back to the sitting room. But as soon as he walked through the door, he knew that Lady Dubb would not be needing any food or drink. She was lying back on the sofa, her eyes staring blankly at the ceiling, and she was, very obviously, dead.

William placed one of the patches from the medipac on Lady Dubb's arm and another on her forehead.

'Diagnosis: the patient has experienced myo-cardial infarction,' said the voice from the box, 'and is deceased. Please consult your surgeon immediately.'

'There isn't a surgeon,' said William. 'There's only me.'

'Do you require Life Support until a surgeon can be found?' asked the medipac.

Life support . . . A memory stirred in William's brain of Mrs Duggan describing how his father had used Life Support on Timber when he carried the dog through the Portal to the hospital on Q'Vaar.

'Would Life Support mean she'd be OK till I got her to a hospital?' he asked.

'Reparative surgery would still be possible within the next hour,' said the medipac.

An hour, William thought . . . Lady Dubb wouldn't be able to travel through the Portal for two hours, but maybe Brin could send a doctor over from Q'Vaar who would know what to do. And it might be a good idea to have some help even before that . . .

'Emma?' he called to the station computer. 'Could you ask Mrs Duggan to come down here? Tell her it's an emergency.'

'Placing the call now,' said Emma.

'And I need to get a message to Q'Vaar, to tell Brin what's happened. Can you do that?'

'Message sent,' said Emma after a brief pause.

William turned back to the medipac. 'So what do I have to do?'

The Life Support system was very simple. It was a silver rectangular box that William had to hang round his neck, and then he had to hold on to Lady Dubb.

'Any skin contact will do,' said the medipac, 'but holding hands provides the simplest connection.'

William reached out to take Lady Dubb's hands and what happened next took him completely by surprise. As he touched her skin, he found he was no longer in the sitting room at the station but standing on a hill, looking down along a valley covered in purple grass that swayed in a gentle breeze. In the distance, a range of turquoise mountains stretched up towards an orange sky, and he wondered where on earth he was.

'This isn't Earth,' said a voice that he recognized as Lady Dubb's. 'It's where I was born. I grew up in that house down there.' She was standing beside him, and pointed down the valley to a farmhouse, surrounded by fields.

'Why are we here?' asked William.

'Well, I'm here because I'm remembering my childhood,' said Lady Dubb, 'but I've no idea what you're doing. You should be in your own memories, shouldn't you?'

'I don't know,' said William. He thought for a moment. 'I think I'm supposed to be giving you Life Support.'

'Life Support?' Lady Dubb frowned. 'You mean I died?'

'Yes,' said William, 'but the medipac says I can keep you alive till we get help from Q'Vaar.'

'I see . . . Well . . . Thank you very much . . .'

'That's all right,' said William, and wondered what he was supposed to do next.

'You need to get back to your own body,' said Lady Dubb.

'Yes . . .' William looked vaguely round the landscape for his body but there was no sign of it. 'How do I do that?'

'I'll give you a hand,' said Lady Dubb, and the next thing William knew something was pushing him sideways and he was rushing through rooms, and places, and wars and towns, and great towering cities and crowds of people, and then suddenly he was back in his own mind, wading through a sea of memories. Memories of himself as a baby, memories of his father taking him swimming and his mother driving him to school, thousands of memories, and he wanted to stop and look at them but behind him Lady Dubb's voice was urging him on, pushing him forwards, telling him to keep going, and somehow he forced himself to wade through the memories until, with a faint popping in his ears, he found he was back in the sitting room, back on the sofa, back in his body, holding the hands of a lifeless Lady Dubb.

In front of him, peering anxiously down, was Mrs Duggan, and beside her was Brin, the station manager from Q'Vaar, looking equally worried.

'William?' he was saying. 'William, are you there? Can you hear me? William, are you all right?'

William managed to nod. It wasn't easy. Any sort of movement seemed to take a lot of energy and most of his energy seemed to be somewhere else.

'Thank goodness for that!' Brin smiled with relief. 'OK, first thing, you'll notice I've tied your hands together . . .'

With an effort, William moved his head to look down and saw that a bandage had been wrapped round his hands, binding them to Lady Dubb's.

'It's important not to break the connection, you see. We need to take you through the Portal. We have to get Lady Dubb to the med station on Q'Vaar. That's where all the equipment is.'

'Can't . . .' William's tongue felt slightly too large for his mouth and speaking was even more difficult than moving. 'Can't go for two hours.'

'It's all right.' Brin was smiling again. 'The

techies have worked it all out. She'll be fine. You just sit there and let us do the work, OK?'

He didn't have much choice about just sitting there, William thought. Even blinking seemed to take a great effort of will, and he waited while Brin and Mrs Duggan bustled around him with a stretcher. It was a clever device and Brin shortened it and widened it before lifting William's legs and sliding it beneath him. The next thing he knew, the stretcher was floating both him and Lady Dubb gently upwards and all he had to do was sit there while Brin manoeuvred them carefully out into the lobby.

In the Portal room, the stretcher lowered them to the floor and Brin slid it out from beneath them. There was something behind his back, William could feel, to stop him falling over and he sat there, wondering how long he would have to wait.

Brin gave him a reassuring smile. 'Everyone's waiting for you at the other end, but we're going to leave it as long as possible before we go, so there's time for a word with your brother – if you think you can manage it?'

Slowly, William managed to open his mouth and speak. 'Why?'

'He's worried about you,' said Mrs Duggan.

'He knows something's up,' said Brin, 'and

although we keep telling him you're all right, he thinks you're going to disappear like your parents did. If you could tell him that's not going to happen?'

William wondered how reassuring it would be to see your brother on a stretcher holding hands with someone who was dead, but then remembered this was Daniel. Someone dead would probably just make it more interesting. He nodded again and Mrs Duggan said she would go and get him.

'Here.' Brin was holding out a glass of something with a straw. 'Have a drink of this.'

William wasn't sure what the drink was but it helped. Almost immediately, he felt the energy coming back into his body. He felt more solid, more real, and by the time Mrs Duggan returned with Daniel and Amy he was able to turn his head and give them what he hoped was an encouraging smile.

Daniel stared at him, white-faced and worried. 'Is she really dead?'

'Only a bit,' said William. 'And no, you can't have the skull.'

Daniel grinned. 'You look really weird!'

'I feel a bit odd,' William admitted. 'Try not to burn the house down while I'm gone.'

'OK!'

William looked at Amy. 'Nice outfit.'

'Thank you!' Amy smiled happily. 'It's a puff-skirt. I think they're making a comeback because –'

'Tell him later,' Mrs Duggan interrupted. 'Lad needs to save his strength.'

It was true that William needed all his strength over the next hour. Twice Brin gave him a drink from the mug with the straw, but it seemed to have slightly less effect each time and William was quietly relieved when he heard Emma announce from the ceiling that it was time to go.

A moment later he was falling through the Portal, falling and falling and . . . not falling at all, but rising, travelling up and up until he was back in the same room only it wasn't the same room because Brin and Mrs Duggan weren't there and this room was filled with people and they were reaching forward and one of them was undoing the bandage that tied his hands to Lady Dubb's, and another woman with long, dark hair was lifting the silver box from round his neck and smiling and telling him it was OK, and suddenly Lady Dubb wasn't there on the edges of his mind any more and he could move and talk quite normally again.

At least he could have done if he had wanted, but he was so tired that he had no inclination to do any of those things, and the woman with the

long hair was smiling at him again and telling him
it was all right, that everything was all right . . .
and he could sleep.

CHAPTER EIGHTEEN

William wasn't quite sure how long he slept, but when he woke he was extremely hungry.

'Giving half your life energy to someone else can take it out of you,' said Uncle Larry as he bustled in with a breakfast tray and placed it on William's bed. 'You'll feel better once you've got this inside you.'

From the shape of the room, and the strange design of the furniture, William guessed he must be in one of the passenger suites on the Q'Vaar station, but the breakfast on the tray looked reassuringly normal. There was a bowl of porridge, a plate of what looked like bacon and eggs, and a very large pile of toast.

'I tried to choose food that was close to what

you're used to,' said Uncle Larry. 'The bread's not as good as yours but this stuff,' he pointed to the bacon, 'is amazing.'

'Is Lady Dubb all right?' asked William.

'She most certainly is!' Uncle Larry helped himself to one of the pieces of toast. 'New heart, new set of arteries, and looking forward to thanking you.' He took two bits of the bacon and folded them inside the bread. 'Because if you hadn't done what you did, she'd have died.'

'I thought she had,' said William.

'I mean it would have been too late to revive her,' said Uncle Larry. 'If you leave it too long, even with Life Support, there's nobody left inside to bring back.' He took a bite of his sandwich. 'As I'm sure you knew.'

'No,' said William. 'No, I didn't.'

'Oh . . . Well, it's simple enough.' Uncle Larry took another bite. 'Your soul leaves your body when you die, but there's still a connection for ten or fifteen minutes, so if you do a quick enough repair, it can come back. What Life Support does is give you another hour or so, but after that the soul moves on anyway, and whatever you do to the body, you'll never get back the person who was in it.'

Uncle Larry patted William's arm, leaving a slight stain of grease on his sleeve. 'You did exactly the right thing! In fact, you did the *only* thing that could have saved her and we're all very proud of you! Now . . .' He stood up. 'I'll let you concentrate on your breakfast, but when you've finished there's a lot of people want to see you.' He walked to the door. 'Get Betty to show you the news feature while you're eating. You'll enjoy that!'

Betty turned out to be the Q'Vaar station computer. She had a voice exactly like Emma's and she showed William the news item in a hologram that appeared at the end of his bed while he ate his porridge.

The report began with images of William and Lady Dubb arriving through the Portal, while a voice-over explained how Lady Dubb, 'famous lone survivor of the *Corinthian*', had had a heart attack and been given Life Support by 'plucky young William Seward', the manager of the Earth Portal.

As Lady Dubb was swept away by the medical team and William was placed on a stretcher, the reporter explained how William, who had recently taken over the station after the 'mysterious disappearance' of his parents, had 'without hesitation and with no regard for his own personal safety' courageously used his life energy to keep her alive for the hour it took to get her to Q'Vaar.

After that, there was an interview with Lady

Dubb, sitting up in bed at the medical centre, saying what a remarkable young man William was and how she looked forward to seeing him and thanking him for what he had done. Finally, there was an interview with Uncle Larry who said that he was delighted that everything had turned out so well, though he did want to point out that all his staff were carefully trained to cope with exactly this sort of emergency.

When the report was finished, Betty asked if he wanted to see any of his messages, and it was these that made William realize that the news report must have been shown, quite literally, around the galaxy. There were hundreds of them, and more coming in, Betty told him, with every brick.

A few of the messages were from people he knew. There was a cheery greeting saying well done from Hippo White, a kind note of congratulations from General Ghool, and a rather nice hologram from Aventa which said simply, 'You toerag! How come you treat old ladies better than you did me?'

But most of the messages were from men and women living on planets light years from Earth, whom William had never met. Some wanted to say how brave they thought he had been. Some wanted to say they had been in similar situations themselves and knew how he must have felt, and some just wanted to say that Lady Dubb was a very special person and anyone who kept her alive and kicking deserved a seriously big thank you. They all had their own reasons for writing but a large number of them, William noticed, were from people who had known his father.

Somewhere in their letters, after they'd congratulated him on ignoring the risks involved in giving anyone Life Support, they would mention that they had met William's father while travelling through the Portals – sometimes years before – and remembered the kindness he had shown in looking after them. It was the first most of them had heard of Mr and Mrs Seward's disappearance, and they would go on to say that they hoped there would soon be news of their safe return.

A message from a man called Napier, on a world even closer to the Rim than Earth, was fairly typical. The hologram showed a man sitting at a desk with a tantalizing glimpse of an alien landscape partly visible through the window behind him.

'Hi William,' the message began. 'You don't know me but I just wanted to say how moved I was to hear what you did for Lady Dubb. The Federation needs people like her, particularly in these troubled times, so . . . well done. We all know how dangerous giving Life Support can be, but you went straight in there. Good for you!'

Uncle Larry came back in at that point, and William was about to turn the message off when Uncle Larry waved for him to carry on, pulling up a chair to sit by the bed and watch.

'The news report said,' the figure in the hologram continued, 'that your parents had "mysteriously disappeared". I'm not sure what that means but I hope they're all right. Your father and I saw quite a bit of each other back in the sixties. I was doing a lot of travelling then and I remember how I always looked forward to calling in at the Earth station. It didn't matter what time you got there, your father would be waiting, ready to greet you, and however tired and grouchy you were when you arrived, a few hours with your dad and you'd be thinking maybe things weren't quite so bad after all. He could do that, your dad! I never knew how. Anyway, I hope he gets back all right – and your mother – and when they do, give them my best wishes, will you?'

The hologram flicked out.

'There's a lot of them like that,' said William. 'From people who knew Dad.'

'I'm not surprised,' said Uncle Larry. 'Very popular man your father. Twenty years in the business. He made a lot of friends. Are you going to have that last bit of bacon?'

William shook his head, and Uncle Larry took the bacon and a piece of toast and made himself another sandwich. He chewed thoughtfully for a minute and, when he finally spoke, it was in a quieter, gentler voice than the one he normally used.

'Did I ever tell you why I chose your dad to be station manager?' he asked.

'No,' said William.

'Well, when old Donald Peterson finally decided to retire and I had to find a replacement,' Uncle Larry said, settling back in his chair, 'I knew I needed someone who was honest, reliable, trust-worthy and so on – but there was one other quality I was looking for that was at least as important as any of those.'

Uncle Larry's sandwich was dripping butter on to the floor, and William put a plate under it.

'A lot of people think managing a station is just a matter of pouring out drinks and making sure there's clean sheets on the bed, but it's a lot more than that – at least it is if you're doing it right. We get some very important people coming through the Portals – planetary ambassadors, captains of industry, government officials – the sort of people who have to make big decisions, and it matters if they come out at the end of a journey feeling tired and bad-tempered. They need looking after.'

'A good manager is someone who knows what a passenger needs almost before they've said it. He has this knack of making things easier for the people around him, he can get them to relax, he can make things . . . *comfortable*. Your dad could do it brilliantly. That's why people liked him. That's why they liked calling in at the Earth station, and that's why they wrote all those letters when they heard he'd disappeared.'

'I think it's a gift some people are born with.' Uncle Larry had noticed the butter on the floor and bent down to wipe it up with the sleeve of his jacket. 'Like some people are good at sports or music, some people are born good at . . . at people. They know how to look after them. They seem to know . . . how they *work*. And in case you hadn't noticed,' Uncle Larry reached out and touched William lightly on the arm, 'it's a gift you have yourself.'

'Me?'

'I can't tell you how worried I was at the thought of leaving you alone with your brother and Mrs Duggan and Amy!' Uncle Larry chuckled. 'I mean, no offence, but what a combination! Mrs Duggan is totally dysfunctional, your brother's mad as a brush, and Amy is downright scary –'

'They're not *that* bad,' said William.

'Oh, yes they are!' Uncle Larry disagreed

cheerfully. 'I told Brin I thought you'd all be killing each other inside a week, but you weren't, were you? Things were a bit iffy for a while, but then you . . . you worked something out.'

'And your family was only the start of it! I was here on Q'Vaar when Mr Forrester came through the other day. That man is the grumpiest individual in the quadrant but I watched him come up through the Portal, grinning like he'd won the lottery! I've had a dozen letters in the last month from passengers saying how much they enjoyed going through the Earth station, and I shouldn't be surprised, should I? Because that's what people like you can do. Even when you shoot them, passengers go home to their parents and say it was their own fault.' There was a slight pause before Uncle Larry continued. 'Which is why I'm hoping you'll take the job.'

'Job?' said William. 'What job?'

'Station manager, of course!' Uncle Larry's eyes peered at William over the top of his glasses. 'I mean, you've been doing it for the last six weeks anyway, so we all know you can. And you seem to enjoy it. So . . . what do you say?'

'I . . . I . . .' William was almost too surprised to answer. It might be true that he enjoyed looking after the passengers and the Portal, but . . . but he could never be station manager.

Never.

'Looking after the station is Dad's job,' he said.

'I think maybe it's time we faced the truth here.' Uncle Larry's smile faded as he spoke. 'You saw the last report from Federal Security. I know it's difficult, but I think at some point we are going to have to accept the fact that we may never know what happened to your mother and father.'

Which just goes to show, as he often said later, how even the best of us can get it completely wrong.

CHAPTER NINETEEN

Technically, Q'Vaar was not a planet or an asteroid, but a moon, a barren lump of rock with some five hundred or so inhabitants who mined the seams of zirconium and platinum that lay beneath the surface, then sent the refined ore back through the massive Trade Portals to the worlds that needed them.

Uncle Larry had assured William that there was nothing interesting about the place whatever, but the first thing he saw when he walked into the main reception room of the station was a view – a real view – of the surface of Q'Vaar with the vast circle of Blue, the gas giant around which Q'Vaar circled, hanging directly above him and filling most of the sky.

It was an astonishing sight and, seeing it, William

understood for the first time what it must be like to come to Earth through the Portal and see a summer's day in England or a rainstorm at night – to see a world where every plant and animal you saw was different from anything you'd experienced before.

At the time, however, there was little chance to stand and stare. Lady Dubb was already marching across the floor towards him, her arms outstretched.

'Here he is! The young man who saved my life! Come along! I don't care how embarrassed you are, I *have* to give you a hug!'

She looked, William couldn't help thinking, remarkably well for someone who had had a new heart put in twelve hours before, though with Lady Dubb he wouldn't have been entirely surprised to hear she had fitted the thing herself.

'How are you?' She held his face in her hands and looked closely at him. 'Inside. Is everything all right?'

'I'm fine, thanks.'

'Yes, you don't look too bad . . .' Lady Dubb took his hand and led him over to the sofa. 'The doctors told me you seem to have kept most of your marbles, which is encouraging. And I hope you know how grateful I am for what you did. It must have taken a great deal of courage.'

William suddenly felt the need to tell someone the truth. 'I wasn't really being brave,' he said. 'I didn't even know it was dangerous until I saw them say it on the news. I just asked the medipac what to do and then did it.'

'Very sensible of you,' said Lady Dubb, 'though I suspect you're the sort of person who'd have done it anyway, even if you had known the risks.'

'What *were* the risks exactly?' asked William.

'Well,' Lady Dubb leant back thoughtfully, 'sharing life energy means sharing minds and not everyone takes to that. Because sharing minds means sharing memories and after an hour in someone else's head you can come out not quite sure which memories are yours and which are the other person's. It's not so bad if you knew each other before, but strangers can find it very confusing.' She looked carefully at William. 'I presume you can remember seeing things in my mind?'

'Yes,' said William. The picture of Lady Dubb standing beside him in the world with the orange sky and the house in the valley of purple grass was still particularly vivid.

'Normally, of course, we'd both be far too polite to mention anything we saw, but I did catch something in your mind that I thought I should pass on . . .' Lady Dubb paused. 'I saw that you know your parents are all right.'

'Oh,' said William. 'Well, it's true that I've always had the feeling –'

'I'm not talking about a feeling,' Lady Dubb interrupted. 'What I saw was that you *know* what happened to them.'

'But I don't,' said William. 'Nobody does.'

'You do,' said Lady Dubb calmly. 'It's a long way down and you're not conscious of it yet, but the information is definitely there. I saw it.'

It took a moment for William to realize what she meant. 'You're saying . . . I know what happened to my parents but . . . I don't *know* that I know?'

'That's about the sum of it,' said Lady Dubb. 'I expect the answer will trickle into your conscious mind eventually, or . . .' She paused again. ' . . . Or I could just tell you.'

William stared at her. 'You know where they've gone?'

'*You* know where they've gone,' Lady Dubb corrected him. 'It's a part of your mind I just happened to share.'

'Where?' said William urgently. 'Where are they? Where have they gone? What happened?'

Lady Dubb opened her mouth to reply but, even before she had uttered a word, William suddenly knew what she was going to say. The answer popped into his mind as whole and complete as if it had been there all along.

'Ah . . .' Lady Dubb smiled gently. 'I don't need to tell you after all, do I?'

'No,' said William.

And she didn't. Because he now knew exactly what had happened to his parents.

'You *know*?' said Brin. 'Are you sure?'

He was standing in the lobby of the station under the farmhouse with William and Uncle Larry, who had just stepped out of the Portal.

'I don't *know* exactly,' said William.

'He has a theory,' said Uncle Larry, 'but it does seem to explain all the facts.'

'Well, that's more than anyone else has been able to do.' Brin combed his fingers through his beard. 'And the theory is?'

William took a deep breath. 'I think Mum had an accident,' he said, 'on the day she and Dad went missing. I think she was out looking for plants or something at the quarry, and then tripped or slipped.'

'We know something happened at the quarry,' said Uncle Larry, 'because of the bag with the blood that the vet found. William thinks she had a fall. A very bad fall.' He paused. 'Bad enough to kill her.'

'Ah.' Brin's face fell.

'Dad must have realized something bad had happened,' said William. 'I don't know how –

maybe Mum didn't answer the phone when he called her – but whatever it was, he went out to look for her, and took a medipac.'

'So he finds Lois out by the quarry.' Uncle Larry had taken up the story again. 'He climbs down, and the medipac tells him that she needs real doctors to mend whatever's broken. If he wants to save her, somehow he has to get her back to the Portal – but time's running out. The medipac tells him Lois has been dead for ten, maybe fifteen minutes, so he has to do something quickly or it'll be too late.'

'That's why he used the Life Support,' said William. 'And then he carried Mum out of the quarry and back to the house and down to the station . . .'

'But if he brought her back to the station, why didn't he take her through the Portal?' asked Brin.

'Because he couldn't,' said Uncle Larry.

'What? Why not?'

'He couldn't take her to Byroid V, because the line was down for maintenance.'

'Was it?'

'It was going to be back up in a couple of hours, but he didn't have a couple of hours, did he? Life Support only works for an hour or so at the most and it would have taken him nearly that long to carry her back from the quarry.'

William thought how difficult it had been simply to move his head while giving someone Life Support, and wondered what strength it must have taken for his father to carry someone the mile or so from the quarry to the house.

Brin gave a low whistle. 'That would not have been an easy journey.'

'No,' Uncle Larry agreed, 'but let's say he managed it. Let's say he got her back to the house and down to the station. Once he gets there, he knows he can't go through the Portal to Byroid V –'

'So he has to come to me on Q'Vaar,' said Brin, 'but he didn't! If he had, I'd have had a med team with him in less than two minutes! Lois would have been in surgery within . . .' Brin frowned. 'No . . . wait a minute . . . Our med team were doing a simulation of an emergency mining accident that day, weren't they?'

Uncle Larry nodded. 'They were round on the other side of Q'Vaar.'

'I could have called them back!' said Brin. 'As soon as I called, they'd have dropped everything else and come back!'

'And how long would that have taken?'

'They'd have been back within . . .' Brin's voice trailed off, ' . . . within thirty minutes.'

There was a silence.

'Poor devil.' It was Brin speaking again. 'There was nowhere he could go, was there?'

'There was one place,' said William.

Brin turned to face him. 'Where?'

'The Old Star Portal.'

'The Old . . .' Brin frowned, then shook his head. 'No . . . no, that hasn't been used for three hundred years! Your dad wouldn't even know if it was still working . . .'

'I think he did,' said William. 'Because Mr Forrester had asked him to find out. He had this idea that you could make a lot of money using the Old Portals and asked Dad to check it out. You know how Dad loved old machines. So if he *had* looked at it, found all the bits were there and still working . . .'

'If it *was* still working,' said Brin excitedly, 'it would solve his problem, wouldn't it?' He had suddenly realized where this idea was going. 'If he went through the Old Portal, no time at all would pass for him, but he wouldn't get to Q'Vaar for three and a half years. And by then we'd be waiting for him and . . .' He looked uncertainly at Uncle Larry. 'You really think it's what he did?'

'That's what we're here to find out,' said Uncle Larry, and he led the way across the lobby to the stairs.

★

The Old Star Portal was both larger and smaller than the one on the floor above. The Portal itself was barely a metre across, but the wall that ran round it was not the gentle lip that enclosed the Portal upstairs. It was a massive construction, nearly two metres thick, waist high, and William wondered how you were supposed to get inside. Huge cables, half buried in the floor, ran out from the Portal wall, and above it, suspended from the ceiling, was another circle the same shape hanging down like the top half of a particularly heavy tin can. There was no immediate sign that anyone had used it in the last three hundred years, but of course there was station machinery that would have kept the place free of dust and dirt.

'How do we find out if Mum and Dad were here?' said William.

'We ask,' said Uncle Larry, and he stepped forward and banged on the desk to his right. There was a cheerful *ping* sound and a young woman in a closely fitting orange jumpsuit blinked into view.

'Hi there!' said the hologram cheerfully. 'Welcome to the entry gate of Star Portal Darius! I am the Portal assistant and may I begin by explaining the safety procedures that –'

'We don't want you to explain anything,' said

Larry briskly. 'We just want to know who was the last person to use this Portal.'

The Portal assistant's smile did not waver. 'Information about other passengers is restricted under Federation law,' she said, 'and explaining the safety procedures is a legal requirement. If I could ask you to be patient while I –'

'I am Lawrence Kingston,' Uncle Larry interrupted. 'I am in charge of all Portals in the fourteenth quadrant and I demand to know –'

'You are Lawrence Kingston?' said the assistant.

'Yes. And I want to know –'

'I have a message for you, Mr Kingston,' said the assistant. 'From Jack Seward.'

'You have a message?'

'I do indeed!' The girl smiled helpfully. 'Would you like to see it?'

'Well, of course I want to see it!'

'If there is anything else you require, please ask for a –'

'Just get on and give us the message, will you!' said Uncle Larry. 'Now!'

The orange-uniformed assistant disappeared and was replaced a moment later by William's mother and father.

Seeing them after so long took William's breath away. They were standing just outside the Portal – at least, his father was standing. The silver box of the Life Support was hanging round his neck and he was holding his wife in his arms. She didn't look too bad for someone who was dead, William thought. She was rather pale and she wasn't moving, but her head lay very peacefully against her husband's chest. Her hair fell back from her face and she . . . she just looked like Mum.

If anything, Dad was the one who seemed to be in trouble. His shirt was streaked with sweat and blood and there was perspiration dripping from his face, but William didn't care how either of them looked. They were there! They were standing there in front of him and they hadn't run away and they hadn't been murdered by a psychopath and Mum had had an accident and Dad had taken her to the only place where he could get help . . .

Looking at him, seeing the strain on his face, seeing Mum with her eyes closed as if she were asleep, he wanted to go over and hug them.

But you can't hug a hologram.

'Larry . . .' William's father made a brave attempt at a smile as he spoke. 'There's been an accident. Lois had a fall – in the quarry – her neck's broken. I've got her on Life Support – I got there in time for that – and the medipac says it's a clean break, so the surgeons won't have any trouble fixing it, but . . . but I can't take her to Byroid and there's no med team on Q'Vaar . . . This is all I could think of . . .'

Mr Seward paused. You could see him straining to gather his thoughts and William knew better than anyone how he was feeling. How the fog was swirling in his mind and making every word and thought an effort that required huge concentration.

'Sorry to land you in it like this, but . . . I couldn't think of anything else. I know the Portal's working fine this end. You might need to check the one on Q'Vaar . . .' There was a green light flashing to one side and a section of the Portal wall opened out like a gate.

'Time to go.' Mr Seward carried his wife into the centre of the circle and waited as the wall slid back into place. 'Look after the boys, will you? Explain what happened . . . And tell them . . .' The flashing light changed from green to blue and William watched as the image of his parents began sinking through the base of the Portal. 'Tell them we love them . . . Tell them we love them very much!'

For a while, after the image had faded, nobody spoke.

'He forgot,' said Brin quietly.

'Can't blame him for that,' said Uncle Larry. 'In the circumstances.'

'Forgot what?' asked William.

'When he recorded the message,' said Brin, 'he should have asked for it to be passed to Emma. So she knew what had happened.'

'Never mind, eh?' Uncle Larry placed a hand gently on William's shoulder. 'Let's go and tell the others the good news.'

CHAPTER TWENTY

'Hi there, Mum . . . Dad . . . It feels a bit odd, talking to you when you're not here, but General Ghool said it'd be a good idea if we did. He said it was important to keep the channels of communication open, and that you not being here just made it more important not less.

'So the plan is that we come down here every evening and say hi, and tell you what we've been doing during the day. You won't be able to see the messages until you get back of course, but when you do you'll be able to look through them all and see what we've been up to. General Ghool said that would be important for you as well. He said suddenly coming out of a Portal and finding your children three and a half years older was going to be a shock, and that the messages would help you catch up.

'I said I thought you'd never have time to watch them all, and you've already got thousands you'll have to read from other people. The story's been all over the Federation News, you see, and people have been sending in stuff from half the galaxy saying how glad they are to hear you're all right and what a clever idea it was to use the Old Portal.

'It'd take you a month just to read all those, so if both of us send something every day it could take you another year to do ours as well. But General Ghool said you wouldn't mind that, so I'm going to go first and then Daniel's coming down to have his turn in a minute.

'I'll warn you now that his news is going to be mostly about body bits. You know he'd started collecting skulls just before you went? Well, he still is, but he does quite a lot of dissection as well these days, and he likes to take out things like the hearts and the livers and keep them in jars in his room. I think that's why Amy moved into the spare room. She said the smell of the formaldehyde was getting into all her clothes – though it could be she just wanted a bigger wardrobe . . .

'Anyway, I said I was going to give you my news, and I suppose the best bit of news today was finding out that you're both going to be OK. Uncle Larry arrived an hour ago and told us the engineers have checked over the Old Portal on Q'Vaar, it's working fine, and he's already booked a medical team to be on standby when you come through. He says the medipac records show how Mum broke her neck and they can fix it quite easily, which is great.

'The other bit of good news Uncle Larry had is that you both get sick pay while you're away and Mr Forrester – he's the head of the Altari Bank – is putting your money into a special account. He says after three and a half years you'll be surprised how it mounts up.

'And while you're away, it looks like I'm going to be in charge of the station. I was a bit worried about that at first. I thought maybe Uncle Larry should find someone with proper qualifications – but he said the best qualification was finding someone who'd already done it for six weeks without too many complaints.

'I hope he's right, but it's not like I have to do everything on my own anyway. Mrs Duggan helps with the bricks, Uncle Larry still calls in when he can and Brin comes over once a week, which is really kind of him. I was worried at first that he was being too kind, but then I noticed, when he does come over, that he spends quite a lot of time with Mrs Duggan. Daniel says he's seen them holding hands. I'll let you know how that one goes.

'I'm usually the one that looks after the passengers, and the only problem there was what would happen if they came through while I was at school – but Uncle Larry sorted that out. He went into school and told them I have this rare kidney disease and have to stay at home sometimes – so if there's a passenger in the daytime, that's what I'll do.

'Life's kind of busy, but we're doing all right. We've shared out the chores so that everyone has stuff to do, even Timber – though I'm not sure we should have put him in charge of doing the washing. He's not good at separating out the delicates, which gets Amy a bit cross sometimes, but Mrs Duggan says it's important he makes a contribution so we live with it.

'And I really enjoy working with the Portal. You never know what's going to come up next, do you? And when you get people like General Ghool and Lady Dubb coming through there's not much chance of being bored! General Ghool sends you his best wishes, by the way. He was the one who told me to stop dithering and take the job. He said if you were here it's what you'd both tell me to do, so that was that really. And when you get back you can see if I've made a mess of it or not.

'We think about it a lot. You getting back, I mean. We've put this calendar up in the wall of the lobby with all the days till three and a half years are up, and there seem to be a lot of days still to go. But at least we know you are coming back. It was a million times worse when we didn't know anything at all. All the same, we miss you. All of us do. Even Daniel.

'We have the photos of you, which helps. At first we just had the ones you'd put up on the notice board in front of your desk, but then we found there were all these others in Emma's memory. Thousands of them. I'm looking at one now. It must have been taken a few weeks before you left, and you're both sitting on the grass beside the fruit cage, talking. I can't hear what you're saying but whatever it is it's making you laugh and . . . and it's good to see.

'So . . . you're OK, and so are we. And when you get back, we'll all be here – me, Daniel, Mrs Duggan, Amy, Timber – we'll all be here, and things can go back to how they were. We're looking forward to that.

'I can hear Daniel coming down the lift. I'll talk to you tomorrow.

'Bye!'

★

William reached forward and touched the OFF pad on the camera, then leant back on the sofa. There were a lot of other things he could have said but that was probably enough for now. And anyway Daniel would want his turn in a minute – William could hear him making his way across the lobby.

He found he was feeling oddly cheerful. It looked like General Ghool had been right again. Talking to his parents, even when they weren't there, really did help. He'd certainly enjoyed it much more than he'd expected, and it had been a chance to say a lot of things he couldn't say to anyone else.

Though, of course, that bit at the end had been wrong. When he'd said how they were all looking forward to things going back to how they were, after his parents got back, he knew that wasn't true. After three and a half years, things could never go back to how they had been before. Too much would have changed. But at least he could try and make sure some things were still the same. He could make sure the farm, the house, the station, the Portal, and the family were still there, waiting to welcome them back.

That was his job, William thought. It was his task to make sure all those things were there when his parents came home. That was what he had to do. Yes, that was what he had to do.

He stood up and as he did so, just for a moment, out of the corner of his eye, he thought he saw his mother and father standing, as they had been in his dream all those weeks before, on the bridge of a great ship. His mother was at the chart table and his father, with his legs braced against the movement of the deck, had his arms firmly holding the wheel. The image was astonishingly vivid, almost as real as one of Emma's holograms, though it vanished as quickly as it had appeared.

But, in the moment that he saw it, William was quite sure that his father had looked across at him, and smiled.